GOODBYE, CHARLI—
FOURTH EDITION

GOODBYE, CHARLI— FOURTH EDITION

•

Diane Petit

AVALON BOOKS
NEW YORK

MYS
P4891go4

PRINTED IN THE UNITED STATES OF AMERICA
ON ACID-FREE PAPER
BY HADDON CRAFTSMEN, BLOOMSBURG, PENNSYLVANIA

In memory of a woman who loved, worked hard, thrived on nature, was an insatiable reader, and who had a passion for writing. Diane Petit left a legacy of several books, 20 years of marriage, and was a terrific mother of three children. We certainly miss her and loved her very much. Please enjoy her work.

—Cliff, Micah, Rachel, and Jeanette Petit

Chapter One

You might have expected her to be hysterical, raving, the perfect caricature of a daughter whose grief had twisted itself into morbid fancy. Elizabeth Waite seemed none of these things. She'd entered her erstwhile familial home with the grace of a prodigal executive returned. Had I not noticed recent photographs of Lizzie on the mantel in a thicket of tony frames, I'd have not known her. Gone were her studious glasses, her too-straight nose, and her lanky, drab tresses from our high school years.

"Kathryn." She acknowledged me with a nod. I detected a trace of disdain in her renovated upturned nose, as if my continued residency in south suburban Landview were a measure of my intelligence or that my peripheral association with "junk collecting," as she called it, made me a party to her steadily delivered, but macabre, accusations.

Squaring off toe to toe with her mother—fine Italian leather to fine Italian leather—Lizzie repeated her accusations.

''You will not get away with this, Mother. Somehow, someway, I know you managed to be rid of him at last.'' She flung back her head, the action of a filly sniffing the wind. ''If it takes every dime I have, I'll prove that you had Father murdered.''

Shadows prevented me from observing Mary Waite's reaction. Not so much as a sudden intake of breath betrayed that any dart of this accusation had hit home. Although the hit-and-run that had taken Gene Waite's life was still an open case with the authorities, there had been no clues as to who might have run down poor Gene. I'd wanted to believe it had been an accident. Horrible, regrettable, yet unintentional. Had it been something more sinister?

I suppose the part of me that was beginning to feel like Typhoid Mary had been telling myself that the death had been unpremeditated. I'd no desire to leave death and mayhem among my acquaintances, regardless of the opinion of certain of Landview's finest. Now I couldn't help but examine Mary—and Lizzie—in a new, speculative light. Had the accident investigation remained open because the police were suspecting murder as well?

Prior to Lizzie's surprise entrance, Gene Waite's final sendoff had been unremarkable. A somber service in a dimly lit funeral home. The scent of hybrid roses battling upstart floral arrangements beneath a room filled with too much perfume and aftershave. The urging of friends to come back to the house where the grieving widow offered a catered repast if not a great deal of emotion. However, there's nothing like a daughter accusing her mother of familial murder to liven things up. The gathering suddenly felt less like shiva and more like a ''suspect party.''

I had known Gene Waite in ''my youth.'' He'd been a laid-back high school social studies instructor, who had taken refuge in our Chicago suburb directly from the campus of Berkeley at its most famous. More recently, my fledgling estate-sale business, Good Buys, had brought me back into the life of this now-deceased inveterate flea marketer.

''What an interesting color, pardon me,'' Mary said with practiced hauteur to her daughter. ''Colors you've chosen for your hair. Am I supposed to notice or remark on the change?''

Lizzie blushed furiously. ''You are supposed to be clever enough to at least pretend to care that your husband was struck and murdered on the highway by person or persons unknown.''

I glanced around the room. The collection of neighbors, fellow ''collectors,'' and business associates of Mary's seemed stunned into acting as nothing except mute spectators. Not so, my Brittany Charli. Charli was never one to dodge a bullet when catching it between his teeth could be so much more challenging. Before I could stop him, Charli, quite gallantly I might add, cast himself between the two women, lest blows be struck.

"Get out of here," Lizzie told him angrily, pushing him none too gently nor easily aside.

The dog gave me one of his looks. "At least I tried to make peace," it said. Effort expended, he trotted over to the gefilte fish on the sideboard and swiped some while everyone else appeared distracted.

Mary's finely manicured hand rose to her forehead for a trace of a moment. "Lizzie," she said, lowering her voice only enough to offer the pretense of discretion. "Have you been taking your medication, dear?"

I made to follow Charli's lead and attempt to intercede. It's not that I'm into everyone else's business; I simply appeared to be the only woman in the room with a height advantage and sufficient backbone to do more than watch. And, okay, I'm not one to dodge bullets either.

Before I took a step closer, Lizzie's hand rose and connected with her mother, sounding a vicious slap. Scarlet spread across the older woman's face.

There was nothing tentative about the way Mary cupped her cheek. Her eyes blazed with real fury. Nevertheless, her voice proved unerringly steady. "Bad form, Lizzie." Her eyes cooled to frigid blue. "I think you'd better leave."

For a moment, I believe the daughter had shocked herself. Lizzie's expression hinted at chagrin, if not shame. The moment passed. Tossing her silk scarf over her shoulder, she sneered. "I wouldn't stay here if you paid me."

Spinning on her heels, she cast us all wild looks. "I'll be back. With the police."

The door slammed in the wake of her departure.

Mary Waite straightened her chin, smiled graciously, and said, "Canape, anyone?"

There were no immediate takers.

Charli, who had already helped himself, trotted back to my side.

My fingers grazed the top of his great head. The police had behaved almost jaded about finding my name on Gene's list of acquaintances. Whether they didn't wish to encourage me in my "meddling" or they had genuinely believed there had been no foul play, I had been unable to surmise. Nevertheless, a brief interview had sufficed, and I'd heard nothing about the hit-and-run since.

In some quarters, it is believed that I can't seem to keep myself out of trouble. Another brush with an active murder investigation had my imagination skittering into prickly territory. The thought of me in a ghastly orange jumpsuit, picking up trash along the Ford Expressway with the rest of the convicts, made me feel uneasy.

Thinking about Lizzie and the possibilities proved as seductive as a baritone saxophone playing in the moonlight. The call of the unknown urged me to create explanatory scenarios in the same manner as I would construct images on canvas—wildly, vividly, with my signature abandon and surprising passion.

Wait until I told my dad.

*   *   *

I needed some air. With Lizzie gone, the room became abuzz with speculation.

"Did she say murder?"

"Why would Mary . . . ?"

"Where's the rest of the gefilte fish?" Someone shared Charli's priorities.

Pressing my way through the crowd in the front room, I gained the foyer. A snap of my fingers brought Charli front and center. As he trotted past one suit and some heavily dimpled knees, I couldn't help admiring him anew. What a beautiful dog. Flowing white withers, generous rust-patterned fur, the sort of fluffy ears that are generally reserved for stuffed animals, and an hourglass marking painting his face, which drizzled monstrous rust freckles down his square snout.

His easy manner belied all that he'd been through. I thought of the Pawlicki buy. Charli was one of the few good things that had come out of that sale.

Since my father and I had given up trying to slenderize the dog, he had retained a solid "husky" body. Nevertheless, to the discerning, his soulful brown eyes conveyed that this was no dumb dog.

Charli's freshly trimmed nails clattered cheerfully against the oak-veneer floor. He canted his head as if to inquire, "What's up?"

"I've a craving for the outdoors," I told him, casting a look for my backpack before recalling that I'd left it in the car. Holding the "perfect little bag," I swung wide one of those expensive entry doors that eliminate the need for a storm door. It hushed open as though it were hydraulic and secretive.

The June sun ducked behind a tide of ecru cumulus clouds, casting the front yard and the street beyond into a dove grey light. It was the sort of neighborhood where, in the fifties, kids roamed freely and street football game boundaries respected no one's yard. A noisy, hopeful community had kept its secrets to itself. Every living room had contained ashtrays. Most folks had kept at least one bottle of liquor to provide a guest with a friendly drink. And the residents had little known that the steel mills, which had promised them good jobs as though the factories were dowry-rich brides, would so sadly disappoint their children, surviving to belch futility at their grandchildren.

Now, Maple Street seemed inhabited by a less casual generation, who expended energy in creating picture perfect lawns that would probably scream ''ouch'' were a bare foot to trespass.

My hand trailed down the Waites' gleaming black wrought-iron railing as I descended the refurbished concrete steps toward the yard. None of this landscaping would have been Gene's doing. Mary's eye had planned the purchase of each flowering plum and no doubt measured the placement of each tulip bulb within an inch. A professional care service would have kept the place immaculate.

I shook my head. ''Gene Waite probably would have naturalized the lawn and grown wildflower gardens to showcase his latest finds,'' I told Charli.

Demonstrating his plebeian upbringing, Charli anointed a rhododendron. A crow cawed noisily from the fringes of a chestnut tree across the street. As if on cue, the sun reappeared, momentarily blinding me.

I heard him before I saw him.

Actually, Charli noticed him first.

Displaying nauseating enthusiasm, my dog romped across the lawn to where a Harley Softail had drawn abreast of the curb. As the rider drew off a gleaming ebony helmet, I stepped forward.

"Figures," I called. "What have you got, microphones planted in his collar? Don't tell me—some 'old friends' have me on satellite surveillance and anytime I'm within thirty feet of a murder accusation they page you."

The forty-something man sitting laconically astride the bike listened with all the expression of a dead fish. Dead fish should look so good. With his craggy complexion and solid build, Detective T. J. Cole cut quite a figure. The black leather jacket was undoubtedly for safety. Nevertheless, it gave him a rakish appearance despite a hairline that had begun creeping north. No one was complaining about Sean Connery's "deterioration" either, I suppose.

I'd strolled close enough to be intrigued by his intelligent grey eyes. They never faltered as he stroked Charli's head.

"Kathryn," Cole replied, after letting me marinate in my own babble. "I noticed you gracing the neighborhood with your Jackie O basic black and pulled up to admire your pearls."

His gaze settled courteously enough at the base of my neck. I willed myself not to flush.

"But now that I'm here . . ." He slung his leg over the bike and put down the kick stand. "Murder?"

"Me?" I stepped back, groping for footing with my pumps. I pressed my clutch handbag to my breast. "Mother," I said. "Mother. There's a mother in there that wants me to locate some baby equipment for her." I made a careless sweep of the house with my outstretched hand. "You know, jumpy dumpies, hot trikes, the works."

"Kathryn," Cole said in that gravely voice of his. He stepped forward and I stumbled on an underground sprinkler. "Some people can lie. Psychopaths, poker players, divorce attorneys."

My eyebrow rose. He'd told me once that he "might have been married before."

"You don't have the gift." He looped his arm through mine and led me back toward the bike. I told myself it had just been too long between relationships. That's why such close proximity to him was unnerving. "Why don't you give me the facts?" he finished.

"I think . . ." I began.

"Don't think, just answer the question."

"Question?" I wished I'd had my backpack in hand. This dumpy purse wouldn't even put a dent in his sanctimonious smile.

"Murder? 'Bogert black' in the afternoon means business is good."

I winced. Handling estates was not grave robbing!

I provided a valuable service to grieving, harried, or overwhelmed people.

He stepped closer. ''Some women wear perfume. Lilies, jasmine.'' He tipped his head forward until his warm breath fanned my cheek. ''Kathryn, you smell of danger. Mystery and secrets. What's a nice estate salesperson and up-and-coming artist doing not buying baby furniture today? Who died?'' The unasked ''and how?'' hung in the air.

Looking down my nose at him—no small feat, we're both tall—I replied, ''Gene Waite, as you no doubt already knew. Do you remember him?''

Before Cole had left for Detroit, he'd attended Landview High School ahead of me. Cole shook his head no.

''He taught social studies at LHS. Since he retired, he's indulged a passion for bargain hunting and sales.''

''Kindred spirit,'' Cole observed, crossing his arms, his voice becoming more gentle. I wondered how much Cole had heard about Gene since his death. His question ''who died?'' had probably been rhetorical. It was just like Cole to give nothing away.

I remembered Gene and his thick belly, generous smile, and overly large ears. He was the sort of man who probably could've emanated good humor in the middle of a tornado, which I suppose teaching a bunch of rowdy high school students is a great deal like.

''Good people,'' I replied finally. A part of me wondered why if Cole were involved in investigating Gene's death he hadn't crossed my path sooner. Might he have been avoiding me? I wondered, unaccountably intrigued.

Before Cole could comment, Charli uttered a low growl. The detective and I turned simultaneously toward the distraction. A rusted Pinto had slowed in the street as curb space had been commandeered by the mourners. The driver, a lean-faced, redheaded man with a spotty goatee, surveyed the Waite house like a potential buyer.

Charli barked once.

"That's not a big squirrel, boy," I told him. Noting the predominance of rust on the compact and bits of oil left on the street behind the car, I added, "Although a squirrel might run faster."

The dog had apparently drawn the guy's attention. He quit looking at the Waites' and peered at us. Cole gave him his cop stare. The stranger hit the accelerator and chugged a few feet before the car switched gears noisily, and he disappeared around the corner.

The detective said nothing. He merely kept the car in the scope of his gaze, probably memorizing the license number.

I burst out laughing. "Cole, you are nothing but thorough when on full alert."

He didn't share my joke. I remembered how deadly serious he'd been the first time we'd met. That time, there had definitely been a murder. I had nearly tripped over the body.

"Everybody a suspect?" I asked wryly, reminding him of our first shaky interview.

A trace of sadness flickered in his eyes. He mounted

the bike and lifted the helmet to his head. "Everybody a suspect," he replied stoically, avoiding my perusal.

Gone was the warmth of the moments before. I might have imagined it.

"Don't let me keep you, detective," I cried over the noise of the kickstart.

"I can't afford to," he yelled before roaring away.

Exhaling heavily, I turned to Charli. "There better not be any monkey business about Gene's death, because I'm really not ready to go another round with that one."

The dog looked at me as though he understood. We walked thoughtfully to my van together.

Chapter Two

A hand tanned by many suns, attached to an arm that retained the grasp of an orangutan, halted my progress. I gazed into the countenance of a woman who could charitably be called "harsh." If at any point in her life Gladys Zimmerman had entertained a kind thought, she'd managed to control it. Her face was grooved by years of scowls, frowns, and avarice.

"Miss Bogert?" she said, in the way that some folks had of asking a question by making a statement. We'd not "formally" met.

"Yes," I acknowledged her cheerfully, disengaging my elbow from her grasp.

Gladys adjusted her polyester suit jacket. The awful carnelian garment stretched across her bulky frame with real determination. Her solid body was centered on top of two barrel-like legs. White nurses' shoes

completed the look. I recalled that when she had oc-
cupied the space across from Gene's at the Flea Market, she generally had worn overalls and folksy hats.
It had taken me a moment to recognize her as his not-
so-good-natured ''neighbor.''

''I guess you'll do,'' she offered, peering sideways
at me.

I stared back.

''Though you are young . . . and beastly tall,'' she
finished.

That was exactly what my high school volleyball
coach had told me when I experienced my first poor
season. She had meant that I'd grow into my lanky
limbs and be a better player. Gladys's obnoxious pro-
nouncement concealed no such hope.

''What can I do for you?'' I asked.

I glanced at the house and spied a cluster of the
flea-market merchants congregated at the base of the
steps. Ms. Zimmerman appeared to be their representative. My irritation lessened; my curiosity grew. Charlie had swung around to my heel, plopped himself
down, and stared up at her as though awaiting an answer himself.

In apparent response to my recognizing the folks
behind her, she said, ''Business. You. Me. Nobody
else.''

My gaze began shifting toward the others.

''Eyes front,'' she hissed. ''You're talking to *me*.
Don't forget which side your bread is buttered on.''

I struck a careless pose and observed, ''Have we
business? I don't recall.''

She scrunched up her button-sharped mouth into a tighter knot. ''We do now, and see that you remember it,'' she snapped.

Somehow I felt less surprise than grief when Gladys shared the group's request. Apparently, Gene had hinted at a real windfall. These people, too, felt that his death was no accident. As they'd gotten the impression that he might have unwittingly accepted contraband merchandise, they'd not shared their suspicions with the police. I can't say that I agreed with their decision, but I understood their reluctance to smear the man's reputation unnecessarily.

Since I'd unfortunately developed a reputation as ''a crime fighter'' and curious ''meddler,'' the group thought I could discreetly check things out.

They'd picked the wrong person to approach me about it. Gladys might be verbal and assertive, but she obviously had no honor. The addendum that she had suggested to their request was so selfish it made my toes curl. If Gene had been murdered, Gladys Zimmerman just rose to my personal list of top-five suspects.

Before I could decline her slimy offer, backpedal, or even say, ''You've got to be kidding,'' Gladys Zimmerman continued outlining her story, her position, and my proposed role in her little drama.

From the look on her face, I didn't think she was used to hearing ''no'' for an answer. I doubted if the words felony or betrayal would even pierce her armadillo shell.

Nevertheless, I was just about to enjoy declining

when a business type in a three-piece suit interrupted us.

"Ms. Bogert?" the fellow asked. A white carnation in his lapel matched the color streaked through his still full head of hair.

Gladys looked as though she wanted to bite his boutonniere off. Instead, she gave him the unspoken welcome one generally reserves for an infestation of termites.

"I'm sorry to interrupt," the man said, clearly uncomfortable. "But Mrs. Waite would like to speak to you before you leave."

It took a lot to make an interview with Mary Waite seem appealing. Continuing to listen to Gladys proved sufficient. I turned to Ms. Zimmerman and, without offering her my hand, said, "Good luck to you. I'm very sorry for your loss." *Let her take that to mean whatever she wanted.*

As we slipped past the group of two men and three women congregated at the base of the stairs, I felt guilty as though I should've taken the time to warn them about Gladys. But with my escort directly in front of me, I hardly had an opportunity. I determined to do so as soon as possible.

I was led upstairs and down the hall. The gentleman knocked at one of the four six-paneled doors, eliciting a firm, "Come in."

Leaving Charli in the hall, I entered a master bedroom, which was flooded with light. Mary Waite stood facing the window, her back to me. I quickly registered a double-poster bed, cream-colored comforter, and a starched and pressed room such as one rarely sees outside of magazine covers. A black and white photograph of Gene and Mary as teenagers commanded my attention from a bedside table. James Dean and Marilyn Monroe? No, but same era. Their young countenances seemed frozen in eternal devotion and an expectation of a bright future.

Now, Mary stood alone. A pair of battered men's slippers peeked forlornly from beneath the foot of the bed as though no one had had the heart to move them.

"Mrs. Waite?" I said, feeling intrusive. I suspected that strangers rarely passed these doors.

She cleared her throat before turning. A certain pinched look around her eyes indicated that she might not be as unfeeling as she'd appeared. Either that or this was extremely skillful black widow. "Kathryn," she said, striding toward me, "so good of you to come."

To the funeral or this little meeting?

"Mr. Waite taught me a lot," I replied, meaning it.

She nearly smiled. "Yes. You were one of his brood, weren't you? Never could keep track of you all." She paused. "He did though, didn't he?"

"Yes, ma'am." I'd left Charli in the hall and still felt the need for further formality. Perhaps I had been better off in the clutches of Gladys Zimmerman. Then, giving Mary the benefit of the doubt, I reminded myself that this woman had just lost her husband. Contrary to popular belief and her own daughter's accusations, the subtle domesticity of the bedroom urged me to think there was more to this marriage of opposites than longevity.

"He was a good man," I offered gently.

She lay her hand firmly on the bedpost. "No one knew that better than I." I thought she might elaborate. She became somewhat curt instead.

Mary strode to the doorway, opened the door, and nearly tripped over Charli. I'd warned him a million times not to listen at key holes. He scurried from beneath her with a trace of chagrin.

The widow seemed to bite back a snide remark. Instead, she commanded in a courtly fashion, "Follow me."

It wasn't a long stroll. Two or three feet. She sighed deeply and swung open the door of what I assume had at one time been the guest's bedroom. Sheer professionalism kept me from gasping.

Every inch of space proved jammed with electronic equipment. I recognized a few vintage televisions and antique radios. Mostly the place was littered with the same kind of mechanical debris that one found in alleys on trash pick-up day. I could see Gene in my mind's eye, cruising the neighborhood and hefting these cast-off machines into the back of his pick-up as though they were buccaneers' booty. Good for parts, excellent for collecting dust, and ideal for testing the endurance of a spouse, this collection of stuff was truthfully junk.

Mary Waite didn't actually shudder. She said dryly, "This was my husband's toy room. One of several I'm afraid.'' Stepping gingerly around a blown-out woofer, she continued, ''I want it out. Yesterday.''

I looked at her askance. Grieving widows generally lingered over their husband's belongings. The dirt hadn't even settled on the grave yet.

Smoothly and arrogantly she slipped past me into the hall. I followed. Closing the door behind us, she said, ''I've endured this situation longer than any sane woman would. I'm offering to hire you to liquidate his belongings.''

She made fluttering gestures toward the downstairs. Her painted fingernails fitted like little pink dancers. ''I could cast the doors open and have that entire brood come through the place like maggots, but I'm hoping for a bit more decorum from you.''

Decorum? Maggots? I couldn't help taking umbrage on behalf of my companions in sales. Besides, clearly she thought of me as one step higher than a maggot.

Part of me wanted to leave her to her daughter's accusations, Ms. Zimmerman's plotting, and her own snobbery. That was my sensible part. The other part, the humane pushover, couldn't stop thinking of Gene.

Before I could reply, she nearly nixed the deal.

''Surely, that animal doesn't have to go everywhere with you.'' She sniffed at Charli.

If she hadn't been preoccupied at the funeral service, she would have questioned his presence sooner—although most folks around here were accustomed to his accompanying me, since my dog was better behaved than most children.

Charli stared back, his big, forgiving eyes conveying pity at her lack of manners.

"He generally does. My partner, you know."

Her hand rose to her brow once more momentarily. I entertained the possibility that a headache niggled behind the gesture.

"Oh, all right. See to it that he's been flea dipped. I'll not have infestations in the house."

My mouth dropped open. Charli's eyes narrowed. Our reaction appeared lost on Mary. She had turned and begun descending the stairs. The lady of the manor expecting to be obeyed.

I watched her skim down toward the noise of the mourners with perfect posture, leaving behind the scent of some exotic perfume. Beyond the foyer, I glimpsed the flea marketers chatting on the porch. Suddenly, the door opened and Gladys barged back in. She made for an end table, picked up a candy dish, and poured the purple wrapped mints into her pocket. I fought a grin.

Turning on her heel, she returned to the foyer and prepared to exit. Her sixth sense must have given me away. She stared up, her beady eyes gleaming malevolently. Saying nothing, she spun around and left.

I'd little time to appreciate the sting of her wrath, and Mary reappeared, apparently noticing my noncompliance. "Ms. Bogert, are you coming?" I observed the grey-haired man in the background looking at her solicitously. What was the story there?

Glancing at Charli, I made a decision. It was the only one I'd probably ever really entertained. I started down the steps to join the widow. To take the job. To plunk myself into whatever was going on. Trouble was afoot . . . and I am so easily bored.

It's probably the nature of my work, but mysteries tend to find me. Maybe it's inevitable that as you settle estates, secrets emerge. Sometimes they're innocent, fun, quirky pieces of information; sometimes they're not. At this point in time, I'd begun acquiring a feel for when I was stepping into "it." Dispensing of Gene Waite's "things" smelled like trouble.

I followed Mary through the kitchen, past a couple of caterers busily preparing trays. Charli seemed to consider giving the ladies a hand, but professional that he is, he remained in tow. At the archway to what I assumed was the basement, she stopped and resolutely flicked on a light in the stairwell. A brassy fixture spilled light over beautiful, knotty pine paneling. The walls hosted a nautical theme complete with framed photos of what looked like an old Waite vacation in the Bahamas. The indoor-outdoor carpeting exhaled the fresh scent of potpourri with each footstep.

We stopped at the base of the stairs, which abruptly left us in a dinky space facing two closed doors. What lay, I wondered, behind door number one and door number two? As if in reply to my unasked query, Mary nodded at the door on her right.

"The laundry room. You've no need to bother in there."

It was then that I realized that the doors and meager

hallway reminded me of drywall barricades dividing the space both physically and visually.

The doorknob on the other room seemed to argue with her. Definitely the road less traveled for Mary Waite. Finally, it gave way. As the door swung free, the unmistakable smells of mold, mildew, and surprisingly, pine struck me.

"Herein lies the great challenge," Mary said, stepping into a room that gave new meaning to the phrase "rec room." A homemade ping-pong table, a pool table, a corner bar, and a basement sofa groaned beneath boxes and bags and more small appliances.

I discovered the source of the pine. A bucket filled with those air fresheners that can be stuck on the wall brimmed full near my feet. I imagined Mary tossing them into the room like hand grenades and Gene banking them into the bucket. Charli steered clear of the stench.

"I couldn't begin to sort all of this," Mary said, stepping carefully around the ping-pong table, which supported the stock of Gene's flea market booth, an impressive collection of comic books both old and new. "Sort it. Sell it. Burn it. Just get it out of here."

Spying a tray of older costume jewelry, I felt compelled to point out, "He had a broad range of interests." So many collectors have but a single passion.

"That he did," Mary said, peering at the merchandise around the room. "Everything from music to tools to toys . . ." She stopped and appeared puzzled for a moment. The central air-conditioning unit kicked in and doused me with a stream of frigid air from a ceiling vent.

"What is it?" I asked.

"That's strange," she replied, scanning the area. "He'd come into a box of those ridiculous Fuzzy Wuzzies. I don't seem to see them now."

"I'm sure they'll turn up," I told her absently. A cameo in that jewelry tray had piqued my interest. I was eager to get a closer look. "I'll keep my eye out for them."

"Fine," she said, dismissing the subject. "Can you start work immediately?"

"Right this minute?"

"Don't be ridiculous. Tomorrow will be soon enough."

So much for the first completely free twenty-four hours that I'd managed to *not* schedule since St. Patrick's Day, when we went downtown and showed Charli the dyed-green Chicago River. I had been planning to immerse myself in the first of the series of paintings I'd begun since my last show. The blocked artist in me leapt at another opportunity to postpone addressing that canvas.

"Tomorrow will be fine," I told her.

Charli looked at me. Privy to all my plans and insecurities, he managed to convey censure at my artistic compromise. I raised an eyebrow at him.

"Excellent," Mary replied, striding to the door. "I'll see to a key, and we'll discuss fees later."

Obviously, she wanted us out. Now. I snapped my fingers to bring Charli to heel.

As I followed, her final remarks came over her shoulder like darts.

"The flea dip. Don't forget."

Fortunately, Mary Waite was preoccupied with leading the way. Otherwise, she might have caught Charli in the act.

In the act of being . . . a dog.

Chapter Three

Grabbing him by the collar, I urged the dog back to the base of the stairs. To my relief, Mary Waite had continued walking.

"Charli," I cried, shaking a finger at him. "Drop it."

With obvious reluctance and not a hint of remorse, the dog spat out a red, saliva-soaked blob the size of a tennis ball. Recognizing it immediately, I picked it up with two fingers. The felt surface proved wet, but the Fuzzy Wuzzy Firefly didn't otherwise seem worse for wear.

"I'm shocked. Pillaging merchandise."

He hung his head, his rust ears drooping toward the ground.

"This is not good for our reputation," I told him.

Good Buys wasn't *that* established a business. I'd only
started a few years back.

The dog rolled over on his back. Belly up, he
pleaded for forgiveness.

I took a close look at the Fuzzy Wuzzy. Stuffed limbs
and features transformed the round toy into one of the
hottest collectors' commodities around. As an artist, I
didn't find the thing particularly attractive. Still, it fit
your palm so nicely that you couldn't help wanting to
roll it around. Reminded me of a "Star Trek" episode
that featured feel-good, hand-sized critters.

"I could pretend you had only meant to inform me
that you'd located the missing toys," I told the dog
kindly.

Charli adores being forgiven. He rolled to his feet
in an instant and pointed his snout skyward, stretching.

Turning, I dropped the Fuzzy into the bucket of pine
fresheners. Tomorrow would be soon enough to hunt
for the rest of them. The firefly was missing its tags
and one arm. If it were representative of the rest of
the toys, this wasn't Gene's secret windfall. I suspected that Charli had located one of the newer
Fuzzes, the ones produced in the millions. I'd little
faith that the missing box of the rest would be worth
much. But who knows?

That was one of the things I liked about estate sales.
All the surprises.

Six squad cars. I peered ahead to figure out what
had happened less than a mile from the Waites' home.
The all-terrain vehicle behind me threatened to crawl

up my bumper. I wished that I hadn't borrowed Dad's compact Saturn and had driven the company van instead.

Charli barked once and snarfed madly at the top of the partially open window.

Suddenly, a boy, who seemed all elbows, knees and guts, shot past our car and dodged in and out of the stalled traffic like a salmon swimming upstream.

''Not a healthy pastime,'' I cautioned Charli.

I could detect no sign of an automobile crash on the road. Wondering whether there had been a robbery, I glanced across the way at the Preston Fly By, one of the latest in fast-food chains to have franchised in Landview.

The activity certainly seemed to surround the restaurant, yet I didn't perceive tragedy in the air.

Before I could leave my car to approach a uniformed officer and satisfy my curiosity, the boy ran back screaming, ''Mom, they just ran out of the giraffe!''

The giraffe?

The child hastened into the car behind me. I watched in horror as the mother, honking and yelling, urged the cars around us to make room for her. Reminded me of an ambulance maneuvering in a traffic jam.

When at last my car drew abreast of the police, I asked through the open window, ''What's going on, officer?''

The young woman wiped some sweat from her forehead and said with good humor, "A break from the usual. *Riot control.*"

At my puzzled expression she explained, "Preston's just got a shipment of teensy weensie Fuzzy Wuzzies. We had to cordon off the street to manage the traffic and the pedestrians."

I glanced ahead and sure enough a line of customers snaked out of the door, down the parking lot, and past the corner liquor store. The queue reached nearly to the stoplight.

When it was my turn to drive on, I thought I recognized someone in that snail-pace line. My spirits did a fanciful leap. This was just what the doctor ordered. A light diversion for an otherwise taxing day.

I stashed the car near the alley by the liquor store, feeling grateful, now, for its size. Setting off at a brisk pace, I set my sights on a particular White Sox cap and some very dark glasses.

As Charli and I strode past, we set off some pretty scary grumbles and threats. Everything from "of all the nerve" to "lynch the line cutters." I decided it would be healthier to take a more circuitous route. Ducking behind what I assumed were the employees' cars, I made my way toward a point halfway to the entrance.

The sun had turned the unshaded area of parking lot into a grill, what with all that asphalt and all those bodies. I felt myself wilting in my black dress. The figure I was approaching appeared dressed more appropriately. Boxy shorts, tennis, T-shirt. It was the dark glasses that tickled my fancy and the person's aura of embarrassment that drove me on.

"Detective Panozzo," I cried loudly enough for everyone to hear.

Admirably, Phyllis "Phil" Panozzo barely flinched. Instead, my former high school volleyball rival and current nemesis steeled her expression further.

"Kathryn," she turned my way. I saw my reflection dance in her lenses. "Butt out."

"Tsk, tsk," I said, drawing closer. "You seemed so bored. I thought I'd keep you company."

"I'd rather eat with a cockroach. Don't you have a grave to creep over?" Charli pressed forward, nudging her hand. Grudgingly, Phil offered a petting.

"Where's Dot?" I asked, not seeing her pseudo-adopted niece anywhere.

"She's at my dad's. I try to keep her clear of mob scenes." She paused, and with only a trace of embarrassment but surging maternal pride, continued, "She likes Fuzzies. She sorts them and counts them. I'm thinking of starting her in preschool next year."

I pictured that little butterscotch ball of vivacity and hoped that wherever she went the other kids had good boxing skills.

Before we could continue our little tête-à-tête, a tide of discord rose behind us. We both turned to discover a ponderous man with an equally stout child beside him. The fellow was going from person to person alternately asking and bullying for favors. He obviously was getting nowhere.

The child, a budding, doughy girl stuffed into Spandex shorts and crop top, whined, "Daddy . . . I need one. I need one now!"

In his haste, the father stumbled into a tall, tattooed Goliath. The other guy shoved him back. Hard.

"Dadddyyyy!" This cry did not seem to be concern for her father's well-being.

"Gee," Phil said. "Somebody stuff a sock in her."

As the father collected his dignity—no small task—he changed tactics.

"Fifty dollars," he told the woman two spaces back. "I'll give you fifty dollars for your place in line."

"Forget it," the woman said, dismissing him with her shoulder. "Get in line like everybody else."

Something seemed familiar about the cut of the man's hair, his unruly black eyebrows, and large ears. At last, I recognized him from a city fundraiser. If I recalled, he was some big business type and the president of the park district.

"A hundred," he said, going to the next woman. "I'll give you a hundred dollars."

Phil's hands had strayed to her fanny pack. To anyone else, she'd have appeared to be a tired customer. I felt her alertness like a humming wire beside me.

The child stamped her feet, her chunky designer sneakers slapping the pavement.

"Daddy, I'm hot. Daddy? Do you hear me?"

Everyone in Cook County heard her.

The inevitable happened. The man reached out to "touch the wrong someone."

"Miss?" His hand barely brushed Phil's elbow before she had her shield out in his face.

"Detective." She nearly growled. "I strongly suggest that you wait in line like everybody else, because believe me, a lot of us are starting to have very short fuses."

His already flushed face turned dark with something else.

"Do you know who I am?" he said arrogantly.

Phil tilted her head. "A poor excuse for a father and a worse excuse for a human being. And if you don't want to be arrested for disturbing the peace, I repeat, Bug out."

His big hands balled at his sides. The daughter stared at the scene with a mixture of shock, frustration, and secret pleasure.

"Come on, Becky," he said, reaching for his daughter's hand. "We'll try the Preston's in Munster."

As the two of them departed, the people around us burst into applause and cat whistles.

Phil seemed a lot more comfortable than when I'd first shown up.

An hour later, I arrived home. The home of my childhood. The Sears Catalog house ordered near the turn of the century. The place I'd returned to after my condo got in the way of a fire. Don't ask.

My father, Hyman "Harry" Bogert, was in what currently remained of the formal dining room. Presently, it was strewn with orange and black bunting, faux-haunted oaks, bales of hay, and other paraphernalia. A cardboard harvest moon hung from the ceiling obscuring the chandelier.

Charli took one look at the scene and attempted skulking past.

"There you are!" Dad called cheerfully. He'd been arranging the scene and a bit of hay clung to his few remaining slicked-back hairs.

The dog cringed and halted. I fought a smile.

"So," Dad said, gesturing behind him, hitching up his pants, "what do you think?"

"I think you're destroying the property value."

"Ah, you." Dad accepted the chiding with good grace. He turned his attentions to the dog. "Come on, Charli. Wait until you see what Jewel's whipped up for this month's calendar page."

The prospective Fuzzy Wuzzy customers must have inspired him. The dog sat down with the determination of all those collectors. He refused to budge.

"Charli . . ." Dad pulled.

The dog held back.

"Come on." My father tried again.

Charli dug in with his front paws.

"Dad," I said, plopping my backpack on the floor by the wall and placing my little black bag on the sideboard. "I don't think he's enjoying this."

With the zeal of a perfect stage parent, my father replied, "What's not to like? A star is not good enough for him? Of course he likes it. He loves being a star, don't you, boy? Our boy is going to be famous. Forget that cat, what's his name. This dog is going to be on every wall. I wouldn't be surprised if he inspired a whole line of Charli products.''

He released Charli's collar. Changing tactics, Dad fetched what appeared to be an orange pumpkin hat, doggie style.

''See.'' He looped the elastic under the dog's chin and arranged the leafy stem so it leaned jauntily above the dog's ears. ''He looks like a mensch.''

Charli plopped to the floor and lay his adorned head between his front paws, abdicating the situation for the time being.

He did look adorable. Nevertheless, I suspected that Dad's brainstorm, his first get-rich quick scheme, had begun as more of a way of keeping Charli and me from moving out. It concurrently put me in close proximity with a certain photographer that my father had been partial to. Somewhere along the way, I think Dad's inner artist had been born, and he was now eagerly leaving his barber shop at the end of his workday to produce this novelty calendar.

''He looks disgusted,'' I countered, leafing through the stack of mail on the sideboard.

A certain envelope seemed to call to me from the mess of flyers and bills.

I could feel Dad's interest as I peered at the New York address. *The Melody Joy Gallery.* Good address. Nice stationery.

Ever since my successful re-entry into the art world, I'd been approached in assorted ways by various people about my paintings. Every contact had been recorded and nurtured for future possibilities. None had felt compelling enough to follow up on aggressively. Until now.

"New York, Katie," my father said, suddenly beside me.

New York. The Big Apple. The apex of art. Broadway, bagels, Brooklyn. Fear shot with excitement rushed through my veins.

"Open it," Dad urged.

A sudden dark thought clouded my enthusiasm. "Did you?" I wondered if he'd been managing my career behind my back. Had he solicited this gallery without my permission?

His hands rose defensively. "I swear, Katie girl. I don't have anything to do with this. If I did, wouldn't it be a nice Jewish gallery pursuing my girl?" Dad was conveniently devout when he felt passionate about something.

With barely trembling fingers, I unsealed the envelope and read its contents.

"Dear Ms. Bogert:

Blah, blah, blah . . . talent such as yours . . . blah, blah, blah . . ."

I felt the paper dampen between fingers as I clenched the miracle letter. Wordlessly, I handed the note to Dad.

"Katie!" he yelled, whooping and hopping. "Katie! This is wonderful. If your mother were only alive to see this . . ."

I let him carry on as I walked somewhat dazed to the front room. My gaze settled on an old still life above the piano. With that charcoal drawing, I'd won my first ribbon in our junior high school art show. The giving of congratulations had been left to my teacher. I'd grown old enough to be grateful for Dad's absences, preferring them to the loud embarrassing entries he'd make when he was drunk.

After he'd gotten sober, it had taken my father nearly six years to get around to framing that picture. By then, the frayed edges had had to be cropped.

"What's all the yelling?"

Great, just great. Gary Andrews must have finished selling computers for the day. My former significant other hadn't exactly wheedled himself back into my life, but he was managing to make his presence known. With a little help from Dad.

A gifted photographer, he'd let Dad convince him to work on this project. For old times' sake, or to be around me? *Motivations*, I thought, *are like piles of shifting sand, supporting each other yet moving with the tides.*

Before I could stifle my father's enthusiasm and maintain a bit of distance from my former boyfriend, Dad had already shoved the letter at Gary.

The surprise that he took too long to conceal and the awkwardness of his "Congratulations, Kathryn, this is quite a coup" urged me beyond my own shock. I recalled vividly his many "suggestions" for improving my work.

Feigning nonchalance, I snatched the letter out of Gary's hand and said as graciously as I could, "Thank you."

Why did this man continue to make me feel like a subordinate seeking approval?

As I started up the stairs, Gary called to me.

I turned and found myself looking into his still-handsome face, his eyes softened with a sincerity that made me feel ashamed of my response.

"Kathryn," he said. His countenance reminded me of the good years, the sweet-roll breakfast, sunset-watching, picnic-on-the-lakefront years. "I mean it. I'm very happy for you. I knew you could do it."

"Really, Gary?" I couldn't help saying, an edge to my voice.

He looked a bit weary. "Really, darling," he replied gently.

Feeling strangely chastened, I turned and headed for my room. Had my belief that he'd undermined my career been borne of nothing except unreasonable expectations and unacknowledged insecurities on my part? I couldn't deny the glow I'd felt in my belly at the word "darling."

I paused at the top of the stairs. Without turning around, I replied, "Thank you, Gary. That means a lot to me." And surprisingly, it did.

Chapter Four

One of its green eyes had been gouged out. The other hung by a thread. Desperate appendages seemed to shiver in the slight morning breeze as it curled around the corner of the back porch. It was black, rounded, and endearingly ugly.

Charli let out an outraged but tardy succession of barks.

As I reached out to examine the Fuzzy Wuzzy hanging by a string from the door frame, Charli gave one more sharp warning bark.

"It's okay, boy," I told him. "I think we've got us a . . ." I palmed the creature. ". . . a Fuzzy Wuzzy Octopus that obviously got caught by the wrong whaler."

Sitting on the steps, I flicked my ponytail of unruly blonde curls over my shoulder. The dog stepped over to sniff the stuffed toy in my hand. He sneezed.

''Not exactly mint condition, is it?''

Charli tilted his head to the side for a closer look. I covertly peered around the back lot, trying to discern any trace of an intruder. Nothing except our undisturbed fence, dahlia beds, and the garage was apparent. Nevertheless, somebody had taken the time to rise with the sun and risk delivering this little round message. I could think of only one reason why. And it had worked. My attention was piqued.

''Come on, Charli,'' I said, standing. As I hefted my backpack, I continued, ''We're due to start our new job today. I don't want to keep Mrs. Waite . . . waiting. Sorry, bad pun.''

As I drove down Main Street past Dad's barber shop, I glimpsed several customers waiting for their turn. I honked at the little cinder-block building isolated from the larger, more modernized businesses. The barber pole hardly made up for the lack of snazzy planters the city had put out . . . except at this end of the street.

Dad waved through the plate-glass window, and I drove on. Landview's small downtown, like so many others, had gotten a face-lift. The city council was attempting to draw customers away from the malls by refurbishing the downtown area with its charming specialty shops. Several card stores had small signs offering the latest in Fuzzy Wuzzies. A house next to Panozzo's Pizza boasted a gingerbread sign designating the owner as the head of the Landview Chapter of the Fuzzy Wuzzy Collector's Club.

''You know, Charli,'' I told the dog, as I drove on.

"I think this is like buying a red car. You never notice red cars until you buy one. As soon as you do, it's as though red cars are on every corner and every street."

I turned at the light and headed south.

"But Fuzzy Wuzzies?" I glanced at the dilapidated octopus on the seat beside me. My instincts told me that it was likely I'd be seeing even more of them than I had before. I sighed heavily. And my instincts had become pretty good.

Parking in front of the Waites' home, I examined the property. From the street, it looked as neat and cultured as Mrs. Waite's bedroom. Plopping the octopus on my dashboard, I lost myself for a moment in the swirl of yellow in one of its chipped green eyes.

In my mind, I saw Gene Waite in a succession of black-and-white stills. Gene sitting on the edge of his wooden desk at Landview High School, leaning intently toward a student who was concentrating on an answer. Gene at my graduation, beaming a smile that made me feel as though the moon were within my grasp. Gene at the flea market lovingly selling one of the hard-bound graphic Batman novels, *Arkham Asylum*. (It was the one that had slapped me in the "snob" with its fabulous artwork).

Suddenly, I imagined Gene on a certain road at a peculiar time of night. I saw him turn at the sound of a vehicle's approach. I watched a puzzlement crease his brow as the car sped closer. I witnessed the shock and anguish on his face as the anonymous vehicle struck him.

''Kathryn,'' someone called.

''Aahhh!'' My hand rose to my chest. My heart beat a steady tatoo against my fist.

Blinking away the vision, I peered out the window to where Detective Cole watched me with bemusement.

''Did I interrupt a moment of meditation, or have you taken to sleeping on the job?'' This with a tad more warmth than he'd exhibited yesterday as he said goodbye.

''I was just thinking . . .'' I peered absently down the street.

''I was afraid of that.''

''Why was Gene in such an isolated location . . . ?''

Cole groaned. ''Not again.''

''. . . at that time of night?'' I finished, staring determinedly ahead as though answers might appear before my eyes.

''Please, not again.''

''What kind of person mows another person down and doesn't even stop to help?'' I was on a roll.

''Kathryn,'' I heard him call. ''Kathryn!''

''What?'' I quit gripping the steering wheel and gazed back at him.

With a face like a summer storm and a voice like distant thunder, he replied, ''I do not want you butting your pretty nose into my investigation.''

I perked up. ''Your investigation?'' Charli stood and wagged his tale as though impatient for the hunt.

My lively heart pitched into another excited meter. Almost ashamed of myself, I felt my spirits rise. There was a crime to be solved and I was ready. Maybe Dad was right. Maybe I do have a gift.

"You have a real gift for getting in my way," Cole said.

"Nonsense," I answered, exiting the car. Charli bounded out behind me. "How could I possibly get in the way of such a paragon of police presence?"

He fell into step beside me, matching me long stride for long stride. Cole stopped.

"I could have you arrested," he stated triumphantly.

I turned and came back sticking my face close to his smug one. "For what?" I cried.

He eyeballed the space between us.

"Assaulting a police officer," he answered.

"In your dreams."

Things grew very quiet, and I became acutely aware of the tension between us. There was an unwelcome warmth to it that felt horrifyingly intimate.

We had kissed. The fullness of his chiseled lips proved mesmerizing. Then I remembered the last time we'd been in this position. We'd both ended up laughing. I wasn't any more sure of my feelings now than I had been then.

"I need to get to work," I said, my voice strangely husky.

A hint of a smile worked his mouth. "We both do."

Mary Waite answered the door dressed casually— loose pants, matching shell top, a chiffon scarf gracing her neck. Reminded me of Lizzy. Her expression didn't change at finding us both on her front stoop.

"Detective. Kathryn. Do come in." She gestured toward the indoors and we entered the house together. I felt strangely like a couple. Cole waited patiently for Charli to step lively before shutting the door behind us.

At the doorway to the living room, which proved spacious and elegant without a large assembly of mourners, I discovered we weren't Mary's first morning visitors. Looking more suave than he had the day before, the grey-haired man sat casually and very much at home in an armchair beside the dormant fireplace. He put aside the daily newspaper and rose as Mary reached his side.

"This is my business associate, Victor Stempniak." She offered no further explanations, and the man calmly shook our hands. I tried to recall what sort of business Mary engaged in. I think it had something to do with finances.

A tense moment stretched among the four of us, which I withstood with curiosity, Cole seemed to generate and the other two tolerated with intriguing, nearly calculated reserve.

"I assume you'd like to get to work, Kathryn, and I'm sure the detective has some business he'd like to share," Mary said, taking charge. "Why don't you and your 'canine companion' begin whatever it is you do? As I mentioned yesterday, I'm eager to be rid of . . . the mess."

Cole and I shared a glance. If I knew him well and

I felt I was beginning to, he was sharing my latest tangent. Was Mary Waite eager to dispose of property lest something incriminate her? I decided that I didn't care for the proprietary hand that Mr. Stempniak had placed at her back, although Mary seemed to take no notice of it.

Nevertheless, the widow had created an opportunity large enough to drive a semi truck through. Before Cole could object or otherwise deter me from removing myself from the gaze of his eagle eye, I said, "I'll be downstairs if you need me."

Mary dismissed me with a glance. The set of Cole's shoulders hinted that he wasn't done with me yet. I figured to make as efficiently a reconnaissance of the basement as I could before he began dogging my heels again.

As I gazed at the bulging contents of Gene's largest "toy room," I figured that doing a thorough search of the basement would probably take about as long as calculating the amount of jelly filling in a smashed bismark.

Charli stood beside the bucket of pine fresheners and waited patiently for me to say something.

"Great," I said at last, wading into the work. Piles and piles of labeled and unlabeled boxes of comics landscaped the table. Those plastic book protectors spilled in a pool in the center and covered a good many of the books like rectangular surgical gloves. "I'll definitely have to get a comic-book expert in on this one." The mess appeared worse than the ReRead

Used Book Store, which had paperbacks flowing like mudslides into the aisles.

Well, I am nothing if not stubborn . . . tenacious . . . pig-headed. Pushing aside a tottering pile of old *Archie* comics, I placed my signature backpack on the table. Where I go, it goes. Inside, I try to maintain a reasonable selection of useful items.

Fishing into its recesses, I pulled out a one-use camera. Before the contents of the room got contaminated further, I intended to take as many shots as I could of the merchandise as it was. I'd never tried this before, but it seemed like a way of taking a thumbnail inventory before any guilty parties or dedicated detectives began rummaging about.

I couldn't resist taking a few close-ups of the case of cameos. My unofficial partner and Dad's special friend, Jewel Johnson, had a particular liking for these. The ones she didn't keep for herself sold easily in her resale store, Jewel's.

The artist in me proved incapable of merely taking simple photographs. I found myself fascinated by the incongruence of the merchandise, the play of the shadows, the meager sunlight peering through the basement windows, and the coronas of dust motes striating everything. I was reminded of Gary as I'd first known him—brimming with enough passion and confidence for both our budding art careers. For the first time, I really felt some kinship with Gary and his photography. He'd been talented. Although I'd given up on my dreams and was only recently resurrecting them, I had never imagined that he would. What had turned him from an aspiring photographer to the world of home-computer-program sales?

Lost as I was in a new medium and in speculation about Gary, I failed to notice where I was going. A sudden sharp pain in my calf had me checking its source. The metal corner of a bed frame jutted like a rusted nail from beneath the ping-pong table. Blood trickled down my bare leg toward the calf-high laces of my sandals. It dripped from one bit of leather to the other like scarlet dew drops off morning leaves.

Hobbling a little back to my backpack where my trusty first-aid kit awaited, I muttered, "Good thing I've had my shots for the year."

Charli hustled over, sharklike in his detection of fresh blood.

"Please," I told him out of fear of his tongue. "Don't."

I looked for a place to sit where I could bandage the minor wound without soiling my dress or dipping its hem into my own body fluids. The only open space I could find was a scored, rust-topped leather bar stool. Hoisting myself up, I crossed one leg over the other and began to dab at the blood with an alcohol wipe.

The cut wasn't deep, just annoying. Leather can be so fussy about stains.

Leaning against the curved back of the seat, I tried for a bit more leverage. Before the second spindle cracked, I knew I'd made a serious error. The rotted wood at my back gave way, sending me tumbling over the four feet to the concrete floor.

"Aaahhh!"

My head hit the floor with a crack. Pain shot through the back of my skull and down my spine, drawing a sheet of black over my vision. I wondered for a moment if I were unconscious. My, how time crawls when you're contemplating a concussion. Charli nudged my side. I felt his cold snout pressed through the cotton.

I wondered vaguely if someone were playing drums on the stairs.

"Kathryn," I heard Cole cry.

"Oh, Ms. Bogert," Mary said with annoyance.

My face flamed, and I scrambled to my feet because my dress was in disarray. I noticed the intent interest Victor was displaying . . . in the room. It wasn't that I craved for men to stare at me. It just struck me as suspicious that someone would forgo an opportunity to do so. What was he looking for down here?

Cole knelt at my side and hammered me with questions.

"Did you lose consciousness? How did you . . . ?"

"Have you been seriously injured?" Mary said, rushing gracefully forward if you can imagine what a swan might look like rushing. At my assurance that I felt fine, her concern pitched to annoyance. "I see you've broken one of the chairs."

Cole ignored her and helped me to my feet.

Victor turned to Mary and said not quite softly enough, "Is she licensed and bonded?"

Someone was worrying about a lawsuit.

"I'm fine," I announced cheerfully. Straightening

determinedly without flinching, I continued, "There's no need for you to stay. I'll just get back to work."

Cole gave me a long, unreadable look. "I'll join you upstairs in a moment," he told the others.

Mary and Victor left, possibly annoyed at either my clumsiness or the detective's dismissal. I was starting not to care for Victor. I wasn't sure why. Cole gazed around the room, his eyes settling on the camera. We both went for it; he reached it first.

"New technique?"

"I thought I'd go for a sort of overview."

"Looking for anything in particular?" His voice remained flat as he surveyed the room through the lens of the camera.

"Not at all," I said, limping to him and snatching back the camera.

Charli offered a short bark that I generally interpreted as "Hey, remember me? I've got something to say!" It must be difficult to be so verbally challenged.

The dog stood near the table where I'd injured myself.

"What is it, Charli?" I asked.

He avoided the bed frame and "gestured" with his snout to some point under the table.

Having ruined this outfit already, I knelt on the dusty floor to see what had caught his attention. I spied a glint of metal taped to the underbelly of the table near the edge. As my focus improved, the metal took form.

I groaned. Sometimes I hate surprises.

Chapter Five

I found myself nose to barrel with a 38 Smith & Wesson. I wouldn't have enjoyed finding the gun anyplace. I particularly disliked finding it "concealed."

Cole knelt quickly beside me. I could feel suspicion waft off him.

"It's no crime to own a handgun," I said.

"I wonder if this is registered," he muttered.

"Of course it's registered."

"He just stored it here so it wouldn't get lost," Cole retorted, just this side of sarcastic.

As he stood and carefully bagged the gun, I could nearly hear his mental wheels turning. My nice little solo investigation was rapidly ending. "Thoroughness," thy name is "Cole."

"I wonder how many people have traipsed through here?" he said, pulling out his cellular phone. "Including him." He pointed at Charli, who appeared positively affronted, seeing as how he had located the weapon.

"Dozens," I said, as he completed his call and request for an evidence technician. "Probably everybody at the funeral and everyone before that," I continued, hoping to deflect him for my own selfish reasons. Once an evidence technician went through here, I'd end up with not only a mess to sort but a fingerprint-dusted mess as well.

"Why don't you call in the crime lab?" I queried, leaning against the bar with my arms crossed. "You are thinking murder now, aren't you?"

He stuck one of those coffee stirrers in his mouth and gazed around the room as though a clue might jump out and cry, "Here I am."

"It would be a stretch. All I have right now is nothing," he said, surprisingly candid. "It could have been a simple hit-and-run or . . ."

"Or what?" Mary Waite had returned with an ice bag—for me I supposed. Her composure appeared as tight as a snare drum.

Cole and I said nothing. "Or what, Detective?" She stroked her throat as though she might be stroking her pitch into nonchalance. "Don't tell me that my daughter has actually convinced you that there was foul play? That I might have wanted to . . . do away with Gene?"

She'd jumped pretty quickly to defending herself. I wondered why.

"You were aware that I was conducting an ongoing

investigation,'' Cole answered, striding across the littered room, closing the distance between them in a way reminiscent of Charli stalking a squirrel.

She made a careless gesture. Offered a peculiar cough.

''I assumed that you were simply conforming to procedures. I never seriously considered that you thought the accident to have been intentional.'' Her complexion turned the color of tired lace. ''Why would anyone want to hurt Gene?'' She turned to Victor, her eyes beseeching support. ''That's the most ridiculous idea I've ever heard.''

The look the two of them exchanged proved impossible to read. Neither shock, nor anger, nor fear. Whatever they were sharing, I knew only one thing. Their interplay had not escaped Cole's notice, nor his interest. I had a really awful thought. What had Mary been doing when her husband had been run over?

With the Waite house temporarily off-limits, Charli and I left, but not before Cole confiscated my camera. I suppose I could've argued about it. I saw little point. With my luck, all I'd probably managed to garner were rotten photographs anyway.

After heading for Kmart to buy two cola slushes, I finally faced the stark truth. There was nothing to interfere with my original schedule for the day. There was no reason why I shouldn't be working on ''Gertrude,'' the first in my series of pseudo-abstract portraits. So why was my van headed south instead of north and home?

Because despite the success of my latest ventures re-entering the art world, despite the possibility of a New York showing, I was once again terrified that my latest vision would prove flawed. That the vibrant original paintings screaming for release from my soul would escape to merely peter and wilt beneath the critic's eye. I am, of course, my own worst enemy.

As I escaped the city limits, I encountered a few less shopping strips, some subdivisions in various stages of evolution, and a noticeable number of fallow fields. Dotted among the south suburbs are generous pockets of forest preserve and relatively spacious working farms. I liked to take Charli and run him in the meadows off the bike path, which ribboned its way through several towns.

Smelling freedom, road ditches, and whatever else enticed him, Charli began pacing at the van window. His tongue lolled expectantly out of his mouth.

''Almost there,'' I told the dog. ''Hold on.''

He'd begun slobbering on the upholstery. Nobody's perfect.

We arrived none too soon at the winding parking lot of one of the oldest forest preserves in the area. Gene Waite had once told our class that this particular land had housed barracks during World War II for German prisoners. Later, it served as a Girl Scout camp. Whenever I visited, despite the streaming sunlight and pirouetting butterflies, I felt much as I did at the homes of the families I served. A presence, either individual or collective, seemed to linger in the land ... the air ... the wind. Although devoid of people,

Sweet Woods teemed with spirit. I felt as though cold feathers traversed my spine.

Shaking off the sensation, I parked and secured the van under the shade of a ponderous oak near an out-house and a water pump. As I stepped from the vehicle and inhaled the cool shade, Charli bounded out beside me. He hustled quickly from tree to tree eager to garner any messages left since his last sojourn.

My apprehension returned. In a cul-de-sac down the drive, near a more secluded pavilion, I spied a couple of cars. Their occupants seemed preoccupied with business of some sort, more than likely drug sales. Not too far from them a Swhann delivery man ate his lunch at a picnic table, determinedly oblivious to their transactions.

"Come on, Charli," I called. The promise of the meadow further dispelled some of the guilt I felt about playing hooky and the creepy feeling that I'd entertained moments before.

As I strode into a mowed area fringed by determined wild flowers, a newly familiar sound grated across my nerves. Spinning suddenly, I glimpsed the tail end of a rusted Pinto. The car chugged beyond the bend, but not quickly enough. Not before *I'd* memorized the license number. Cole would be so proud of me.

Sitting cross-legged on a boulder, I pitched a rock to Charli, which he fetched with true doggie exuberance. When fetching, he's never picky.

"Why would someone who was interested in Gene

be tailing me?'' I said to myself, squinting against the blaring noon sun. I felt sure it was the same Pinto I'd noticed yesterday. Coincidence? I don't think so.

Charli handed off the rock to me and waited. I hefted it a good distance.

They say a murderer always returns to the scene of the crime. Was the man I'd just seen the one who'd run Gene over? The forest preserve was close enough to the curving road where Gene had been killed to qualify as shared territory. Surely such a distinctive vehicle would've left tell-tale impressions at the site of the accident, I speculated. A deposit of rust, perhaps. Maybe not.

A tremendous blue bug skittered in and out of the lee of a nearby boulder. Its iridescent ultramarine color proved so distinctive that I found myself fascinated by its progress. It ran out and in, seemingly for no reason. Of course, it must have had a reason, perhaps many reasons. I simply was oblivious to it.

Gene's death, this case—now it's a case—was like that bug's trail. People moved in and out for no apparent reason or for far too many reasons.

Mary Waite. Had she hired someone to kill her husband because she'd finally had enough of their lifestyle? Was she interested in someone else? That brought me to Victor Stempniak. He clearly had a more than friendly interest in Mary. Was the feeling mutual? Where was *he* the night Gene was killed?

Charli had yet to return from the bramble of weeds the rock had landed in. I stood and stretched, enjoying the sensation of my flesh being baked by the sun.

Striding through a morass of grasses and prairie flowers, I wished for my Nikes. It was a good deal past dumb to go hiking in these blood-stained sandals. I guess sometimes I just like to live on the wild side.

Walking along, I could imagine myself on a Greek island heading for the sea. My beautiful art studio, which looked over the aquamarine water, awaited my return. An easel. An array of paints, canvasses. Seductive breezes and ripe, fragrant local fruit.

The second before I dispelled the vision I thought I might have glimpsed Gary preparing lunch in the kitchen of that Greek studio. Nah.

''Charli!'' I called. Several gangly sumacs bared my way. Stepping around them, I found the dog, stark-still and intent as only a hunter can be. If he sensed my arrival, he offered no sign of it. I preferred letting him finish his war of wills. A squirrel poised fear-frozen a dozen yards away. There was something nearly spiritual in Charli's patience, majesty in his countenance.

Had someone waited just this way for Gene on that lonely road? Could it have been Lizzie? Maybe she wasn't as successful as she appeared. Perhaps she was looking for an inheritance. She may have wanted to cast suspicion on her mother to eliminate her as an heir. What sort of estate did Gene leave after all?

The squirrel lost. He broke and ran, scurrying for safety in the closest maple. Charli tore after him. Would have gotten him, too, if I hadn't called him off at the last moment. Consequently, the dog stood on his hind legs staring up the tree at his prey. The squirrel chattered its success down the branches.

"Sorry, Charli," I told him, reaching his side. "I'm just a pacifist at heart."

I don't think he felt truly disappointed. After all, it was the chase that mattered. Speaking of which, it was time we checked out another suspect. Personally. I knew just where to find her and I wasn't looking forward to it.

When I was a girl, I had somehow thought that a "flea market" was a sort of infested open-air fruit stand except on a grand scale. As I outgrew such delusions, I harbored the belief that they were like huge garage sales, selling a plethora of second-hand goods. Perhaps some of them are. Not so Santa's Super Shop, which lay just across the stateline in Indiana.

The Super Shop was more a mall than a yard sale. Some of the vendors had worked their booths for nearly fifteen years. Their stations sported such permanent accouterments as glassed-in wooden cabinets, chain-link enclosures for locking up, and a territoriality that would've made an alpha wolf proud.

Gene and some of the senior marketers had moved to the newer air-conditioned wing of the market after it had opened. The rent was higher, the green-and-red paint job more oppressive, but there was better ventilation, more room, and even windows far away as they might be.

I paid my seventy-five-cent admission to a tired

clerk wearing one of the Shop's signature elfin hats, a floppy felt affair in red or green. The clerk's pom pom appeared more dilapidated than my "spider gift." The warehouse's high ceiling prevented the shoppers' decibel level from being a din.

Leather imports. Victoria's Secret and Bath and Body Works. Win Chun and Sons Jewelry. Fuzzy Wuzzies. African caps and caftans. Crystals and incense. Fuzzy Wuzzies. Mel's hardware. Chicago T-shirts. Disney videos. Fuzzy Wuzzies.

As Charli and I wove through the crowd, I felt astonished that I had paid so little attention to the little novelties before. Stopping at one station, I noted prices that ranged from $5.99 to $12.99, and up to $45 for Fuzzies that had original boxes or tags. Little plastic tag protectors hung for sale on turnstiles like key rings.

"Hello, darling girl," a slender, woman with stark-ebony hair, pancake-covered wrinkles, and strangely stylish Bermuda shorts hailed me. She stepped to the side of her table of toys. "Aren't you a darling? What you need is a bit of luck, eh?"

Possibly noticing my doubtful look, she shifted gears. Gone was the modern-day gypsy, almost. "Darling girl, do you know the story behind the Fuzzy Wuzzies?"

Charli plopped himself down at my feet. He loves a good tale, no pun intended. Figuring that I might garner some useful background information, I grew attentive.

Her beringed hands cast in front of her face as though moving away mystic clouds to reveal the details. In an enthralled voice, she told me the history of fads in less than five minutes. First there were pet rocks, then there were Beanie Babies, and now Fuzzy Wuzzies. Fuzzy Wuzzies were the brainchild of an ex–Franciscan monk who had literally designed the prototypes from a metaphysical/scientific standpoint as his contribution to a new peaceful world consciousness.

The shape, material, and density of the toy was intended to massage vital acupressure points in your hand as you rolled the toy on your palm. The whimsical animals had caught on quickly and soon their medicinal properties were completely obscured by New York marketing strategies, which touted their value as "collectibles."

After the company became publically owned and run by a savvy board of directors, the monk was reduced to a disillusioned figurehead. However, when the company went so far as to come out with its first singing Fuzzy, the monk sold out his shares and disappeared in disgust at the travesty that had overtaken his vision.

"They say he bought an island in the South Seas, darling." Her eyes narrowed, creasing the heavy makeup around them into unsightly trails of spent youth.

"Here, darling girl," she took my hand and placed a dog Fuzzy in it. Amazingly the toy, despite its circular shape, had fluffy ears, a stub of a tail—a Brittany Fuzzy!

"Try this one." She demonstrated what she called

"working" the toy for serenity, rather like milking a cow, I observed.

"How much?" I found myself saying.

"Oh, for you, darling, a special price . . . twenty-five dollars." Her head canted expectantly to the side.

After a couple of minutes of delightful dickering, I walked away the proud owner of my first Fuzzy—*Britt*. Charli eyed the thing with interest and finally jealousy, before returning his attentions to being inconspicuous. There are always management types around who don't care for dogs inside their establishments and would gladly cast his furry hide into the street.

Down a wide aisle, as thick with people as a New York boulevard, I headed toward Gene's former booth, which lay in the far southeast corner of the building. A tall man with a shaved head and princely features attempted to arrange his merchandise—towers and wood crates of shrink-wrapped CDs—while a boar of a woman harangued him unmercifully. The fellow, who could have doubled for a heavyweight boxer, maintained his temper admirably. He appeared to barely notice her as he bopped and boogied his way around his territory to the strains of a hard-rock tune. A neon sign hung behind him blaring *Discount CDs* in chartreuse letters.

I stood for a moment and observed the woman. It was when she turned around, went to the booth behind her, and emerged with a tire iron that I felt compelled to act. The only thing I could think of was to distract her. I threw the first thing I could reach, which in this case was already in my hand—a Fuzzy Britt.

The Fuzzy beamed her in her flat, broad nose. As she turned to me, I noticed the broad tattoo on her bicep. I couldn't make it out. When it comes to tattoos. I'm completely illiterate.

Whether the CD man had been aware of her approach and only chose to react as her attention turned to me, I didn't know. I did feel appropriately grateful for his next actions.

Charli and I watched dumbfounded. In a flash, the man lifted a CD and flung it like a boomerang. It whisked past us and clanged against the iron before its plastic case cracked and it fell to the floor. This time the woman stopped.

"Smashing Pumpkins!" she cried, staring in horror at the damaged CD. "Some kindofasewer *you* are of good music!" She placed the iron against the leg of her merchandise table and leaned to pick up his "weapon." It was then that I noticed a possible reason for her anger. Our mutual assailant ran Betty's CD Booth.

"Connoisseur?" the other man replied. I detected a bit of New England in his voice.

"Yeah, that," she answered.

Arms akimbo, she bore down on him again. This time she appeared to be more annoyed than violent.

"I don't know why the stupidbunchaidiots that run this place keep putting people selling the same . . ."

"Quality merchandise?" I offered, stooping to retrieve my poor Britt. Thankfully, he was no worse for the wear. Charli had taken to sniffing the tire iron.

"Yes," she replied, wrapping a bit of dignity about her like a shawl.

"Because, O Articulate One, they wish to accommodate the customers," the CD man said as he grabbed his CD and prepared to relabel it for sale in his "used" section.

She narrowed her eyes as though trying to decide if "articulate" were a putdown. Thinking to make friends and snitches, I steered her toward her booth and engaged her in a commercial enterprise—the purchase of an old Frank Sinatra CD. Dad loved Ol' Blue Eyes, and I suspected that such merchandise would soon be hard to find.

"That's a wonderful selection you got there," the lady told me. "It's oneofakind."

"It certainly is." I tilted my head toward her competition. "What's the story there?" I asked.

She glared at the man who once again seemed to be setting up shop, oblivious to her. "Ah, the money-grubbingnogoodpigheads that own this place. They always give you a problem. I'll show him." She shook a pudgy fist at the other guy. "I'll sell circles around him."

"Does that happen often?" I asked, scanning the aisles for other pockets of similar goods.

"Often enough," she answered. "Sometimes it works. Sometimes it don't."

She nodded at some Korean-American girls selling cosmetics.

"Those two," the woman told me. "They practically share the space."

"But everyone isn't like that?" I asked carelessly. I flipped through the case in front of me as though planning another purchase. She laughed, or perhaps a wildebeest had given birth under the table.

"No," she answered, staring hard at Charli, who returned the discourtesy.

Sometimes a bit of luck drops into your lap like linguini off your fork. Today my pasta proved delicious. The woman went on to tell me of the most notorious feud in "Santa Land." Apparently, two comic-book vendors had worked face to face further down the aisle. My new friend confessed that she'd learned the tire-iron bit from the more aggressive— did I say nastier?—of the two.

I wasn't surprised to learn the identity of the competitors.

I was surprised to turn and find that Charli had slipped away into the crowd and disappeared.

Chapter Six

I expected to catch up with Charli and find him in handcuffs or paw cuffs or whatever. Instead, I traced him to a neat little pet supply where he'd encamped like a Norseman and was being fed pig ears by his newly acquired "vassals." The vassals in question were two lovely girls who refused to accept payment when I yanked my recalcitrant dog away from that glorious bin of dog treats.

It took a bit of maneuvering to haul him back to our original destination. Nevertheless, I arrived at last at the second booth on the end—The Comic Shop. This was Gladys Zimmerman's pride and joy. I discovered her ensconced behind a table loaded with both new and used books. Hanging above her head as though it were a menacing cloud, a sign read DO NOT REMOVE COMICS FROM PLASTIC BAGS!

As I glanced across from her, I noted a Korean woman patiently selling herbs, teas, and such in what would have been Gene's old space. The establishment had certainly wasted no time in replacing his bit of rental income.

Gladys glared at the newcomer. Observing her off guard, I decided she appeared as perfectly unpleasant as always. How anyone in such well-worn overalls and such a charming straw hat could look so unwelcoming was a mystery in itself. I couldn't help wondering how any customer dared approach her at all.

She noticed me before I had quite decided which tack I was going to take to elicit information from her.

"Come at last, have you?" she said, looking askance at my getup. I'd yanked back my wayward blonde hair, but my Grecian dress had taken a beating and, of course, those sandals would never be the same. I must have looked quite the bum.

I urged Charli to a down stay, which he willingly complied with. Sucking up after his latest escapade no doubt.

Smoothing on the perfect expression—hungry but not overly, remorseful but not abject, and deceitful but only reluctantly—I replied, "Seems I have." My habit of mimicking other people's patterns of speech could sometimes prove an embarrassment. She didn't appear to notice. What I assume was a grin turned her face into something truly ghastly.

Rubbing her fingers together, she nearly cackled, "Money talks. Smart girls listen."

She gestured me closer. At the same time, without

taking her eyes off me, she slapped the hand of a potential young buyer who had made as if to open one of the packaged comics. Her weapon, a wooden backscratcher, whisked out and back like a lizard's tongue.

"Seventy thirty," she said shrewdly. A telltale gleam in her eye told me that she was speaking of profit percentages from our proposed "partnership."

I tipped my nose higher. One must go through the motions.

"Fifty."

"You're out of your mind!" she sputtered. "I'm the boss."

"I'm doing the job."

"Not yet you're not!"

"Not at seventy thirty," I replied smoothly, glancing at a neat display of new miniature Classic Comics. Ah. Before there was *Les Mis* there was *Les Miserables* in Classic Comics form. My intro to fine literature.

She dismissed me with a wave. "I don't need you anyway."

The echoes of the vendors and crowd filled the silence that followed like Muzak in an elevator. I pulled a slow smile, tilting my head to the side. "I think you do."

If she could have stamped her feet, she would have.

"Sixty-five, thirty-five," she said at last.

Someone passed us with cotton candy. Its scent sweetened her offer.

"Fifty." I stood my ground. Charli had watched the exchange with the interest he reserves for fine dickering. If a dog could look both intelligent and smug, at this point he did.

"Sixty forty," she said, gritting her teeth. "That's final."

I paused long enough to churn her stomach contents. "Done," I replied finally.

She sat back in her padded rocker, the obvious equivalent of her office chair, and regarded me with triumph. I let her have her moment. Adopting a conspiratorial whisper, she asked, "So did you find anything?"

"I may have," I answered, tiptoeing my fingers across the wooden surface of her table.

"How much is this?" a pimple-faced teenager asked, pointing to a new comic.

She snapped the price at him. He winced but paid the money. I presumed he was a regular who was accustomed to her manner. *I* wouldn't have bought garden manure from her.

Time for the denouement. "I may have," I said smoothly, "had I known exactly what I was looking for. As you were not specific, I'm afraid that I can't really tell you that I found what you're looking for."

I lifted an eyebrow as she called me some names, which I hadn't heard in a while. The CD man noticed and shot me a glance that read, "Want me to help out?" I shook my head.

"Sticks and stones," I replied nonplused, picking up that *Les Miserables* classic and leafing through it. When she didn't reply, I added conciliatorily, "Surely you can appreciate that I need to know exactly what you think this windfall was? You do know, don't you?''

She considered my offer, her gaze never leaving mine. I could nearly smell her annoyance. ''Fuzzies,'' I think she might have mumbled.

''What?''

''Fuzzies,'' she replied, as though I were deaf, stupid, or both.

I burst out laughing. I couldn't help it. Gladys did not appreciate being laughed at.

''Look around,'' I said with a sweeping gesture. ''They're everywhere. I realize that people like them, but how much money could we really be talking about?''

This time, Gladys looked smug. I felt as I had moments before my third-grade teacher used to announce my spelling-test grades to the entire class. Third grade had not been a good year for spelling.

She beckoned me closer with her index finger. ''The fourth edition,'' she whispered.

''The what?''

''The fourth edition.'' Her eyes burned bright with the lure of contraband and cash. ''A full collection of the earlier Fuzzies in good condition is worth plenty, but a full collection of the fourth edition is worth more. Sales weren't good. The manufacturers thought the fourth one would be the end of it, so only a small number were made. It was after the fourth edition came out that folks got the picture that the little nasties would be hot. They produced twice as many for the fifth edition. A whole set of those fourths would be worth big bucks to the right buyer.''

I couldn't help believing her. Collectibles are a peculiar trade. She could be right. Within two years,
Fuzzy Wuzzies might be worth little except for the
ones that no one thought to buy—like this fourth edition she was speaking of.

"How would Gene have come into that?" I said,
leaning forward, feigning interest in a packaged *Jug-
head* comic from 1968.

It was Gladys turn to appear puzzled. "I'm not really sure. Just know he did. Overheard him talking on
the phone arranging for the pickup. It wasn't like Gene
to be accepting funny goods," she added speculatively. "I figure it got him killed."

For a moment, I thought perhaps her interest to be
more in line with the rest of the marketeers—to clear
Gene's reputation. Then she said, "His loss, our gain."

"Yeah," I agreed, the words sticking in my throat.
"His loss, our gain."

I could barely wait to be free of Santa's Super Shop.
The huge blow-up Santa on its roof wobbled in the
breeze like a drunk. The paint worn off his beard gave
him an unappealing jaw line.

I've never been a good liar, and my play-acting had
cost me plenty. The ulcer I'd once nearly developed
seemed to have metamorphosed into a tension
headache.

I drove straight home. My skin itched, probably
from my sojourn at Sweet Woods. My sandals were
falling apart, and my headache had come to stay.

Charli slunk into the house as though he were expecting to be waylaid by Hymie ''The Calendar Man.'' Poor dog. Life had been much simpler for him when all he'd had to worry about were doggy diets.

''He's not here,'' I told Charli. Glancing at the clock, I added, ''He won't be home for a few more hours.''

The dog's ears perked up. He accompanied me to the kitchen with a sprightly gait. While I rummaged in the freezer for an ice pack for my head, Charli made for his water dish.

Clang!

The metal dish must have been empty. He'd picked it up and dropped it on the floor to request a drink. I moaned, my hand rising to my forehead.

''Just a minute. If you drop that thing again, you're going to find out what it feels like to be a fur coat.''

He plopped himself down with his head between his paws and looked absolutely pathetic and adorable. I felt like a heel.

With the ice pack wrapped in a towel and pressed against the ache in my head, I refilled his bowl. To the sloshing of his drinking I located some aspirin. I took the time to slash a note across the message board: LET ME SLEEP. HEADACHE. LOVE.

''Come on,'' I said, juggling a bottle of medicine, a glass of water, the ice pack, and a box of crackers to hold the pills down. Upon reaching my bedroom, I arranged my pharmacy on the desk and popped some pain relievers. After shedding my clothes, I forsook a shower and cast myself on the day bed with a groan. The stick-on constellations that swept across the ceiling made my head feel as if it were swirling.

"This has been a very long day," I told the dog. I heard him curl up on the floor beside me right before I fell asleep.

The soft whirring of the central air conditioner was the first thing I heard. Somewhere on the block children played Freeze Tag. The aroma of freshly mowed grass confirmed that I'd slept deeply, through the racket of a working lawn mower. I let my hand trail over the edge of the bed and Charli, obediently, lifted his head for a petting. Waking to a dog can be such a fine thing. Once again I felt grateful to have the dog in my life. He was as loving as any man and frankly shed a lot less.

It took a minute for the peace and suburban quiet to fully register. Something was not right. The clock read 7:30 P.M. I didn't hear anyone in the house. Dad should have been home by now. Jewel should have stopped by. Her nightly seven o'clock visit was as reliable as a Timex watch.

I took a quick, brisk shower and threw on a purple tube top and a fabulous sarong that a friend had given me. My headache was gone and I could tolerate a ponytail without wincing.

"Dad?" I called, skimming down the stairs.

No answer.

"Dad?" A look into the dining room revealed

Charli's Oktoberfest still in residence. I was about to head for the kitchen when Charli tipped me off. We walked into the living room together. My father was seated in his wingback recliner, reading glasses perched on his nose. A copy of the latest E. L. Larkin mystery appeared nearly finished on his lap.

Keeping him company, Gary sat on the sofa watching the Cubs play baseball on television. The volume was as subdued as the mood in the room. This, no doubt, accounted for my not having heard it. Gary met my gaze and controlled his glance of admiration at my getup. Nevertheless, I felt a pleasant flush and a decidedly feminine response. I hadn't exactly dressed for company. We took turns shifting our attention to my father, who remained intent on his book, although I noticed at this point that he hadn't turned a page.

Before I could ask any questions, the doorbell rang. Dad shifted in his seat but didn't rise. Jewel Johnson, having let herself in, came to the doorway toting her pie carrier. Her forehead shone as though she'd struggled to get here.

"I'm sorry I'm late," she said agreeably, putting the pie on the sideboard. "John needed some help organizing the data from the curriculum committee."

Although she had taken an early retirement, Jewel had allowed herself to be hired for the summer as a teacher. A former colleague, John Wells, who was now principal at the high school, had asked her personally to help him out. It seemed as though her obligations to the job were consuming more and more of her time.

The silence in the room was complete. Even Charli seemed to hold his breath.

Jewel sighed and stepped over to where my father now very meticulously turned a page. Leaning over, she planted a kiss on his balding head. Her newly highlighted hairdo gleamed youthfully in the lamplight. The makeover I'd helped orchestrate earlier this year had done wonders for her self-esteem. While she'd always been confident of her diverse abilities, which ran from carburetor repair to quiche preparation, she'd never felt secure in her physical appearance. That had changed.

Still, she might have been kissing a cabbage for all the response she received.

Eventually, my father looked up. He looked at the clock. He looked at his watch. He closed his book, took off his glasses, and said, ''Oh, are you late? I hadn't noticed.'' His attempt to stare her down was thwarted by her brown eye. It drifted a little. The blue one held steady and looked slightly amused.

''Hello, Kathryn. Hello, Gary,'' Jewel said, obviously deciding to ignore Dad's sour mood. Gary stood looking nauseatingly sexy in a pair of chinos and an ecru shirt. They shook hands amiably.

''Ms. Johnson, it's nice to see you.'' Gary managed to sound polite instead of obnoxious.

''Please, call me Jewel,'' the other woman pressed. Dad made some sort of harrumphing sound.

''What is it, Hymie?'' Jewel said wearily, turning.

'' 'What is it,' she asks me?'' Dad answered, standing and removing his glasses. ''She waltzes in . . .''—

he checked his watch—''. . . thirty-three minutes late, and she wants to know 'What is it, Hymie?' ''

Jewel fought a smile and glanced at the wall clock. ''Thirty-four minutes, actually,'' she said.

''Thirty-four.'' Dad stood corrected.

Gary and I shared a look. We both seemed equally *thrilled* at being bystanders for one of Dad and Jewel's rare tiffs.

Placing his book nonchalantly on the end table by the chair, Dad continued, ''I'm sure *John* doesn't mind if you're late. I'm sure John doesn't object to anything you do.''

''As a matter of fact,'' Jewel answered, straightening, ''John does seem to appreciate my help very much.''

I couldn't watch anymore. Dad had assured me that he would propose to Jewel—soon. I'd warned him that if he didn't stake a claim someone else would.

''The pie smells fabulous,'' I said, cheerfully. ''Do you mind if Gary joins us?''

Unclear whether I truly wanted his company or needed another body in the house, I startled myself with my invitation.

''Of course not,'' Jewel replied, her manners overriding her emotions. ''Why don't we have dessert? Some of us seem to need a little blood sugar.''

Dad grumbled but allowed her to hook her arm in his. I heard him say as we went to the kitchen, ''I was worried about you. You might have been hurt.''

The storm seemed to have blown over in the time it took the four of us—five if you count Charli—to traipse the hall. Our dog nightly waited for the miracle of miracles—a slice of pie to slip to the floor, his territory. Night after night, he was reduced to scavenging crumbs.

Gary, who had carried the pie, placed it in the center of the table. Then he helped me locate dishes and cutlery. As I glanced at him out of the corner of my eye, the daydream of that Greek island returned. I couldn't help remembering how skilled his hands were, so artistic.

"You look beautiful tonight."

"What?" I replied, caught wool-gathering.

"Like a pagan princess returned from a festival in the pines."

He reached over and tucked a bit of my hair behind my ear. The gentle maneuver brought his face distressingly close to mine. I found myself looking at the neat contour of his lips. I found myself remembering. . . . wondering.

My eyes stayed determinedly open as his lips met mine. Then it felt my lips had met their perfect match, returned home. My eyes drifted blissfully shut. This sweet pressure was nothing like the aborted kiss I'd shared with Cole.

We pulled away at the same time. The knot in my throat felt as though I were swallowing a golf ball. This couldn't be happening. Not again. I couldn't still love Gary! His kisses were simply a template by which I measured all others. That was all.

Gary stared at me and I found myself tormented by

the golden highlights in his hazel eyes, which had turned dark with emotion. Had he looked smug, I'd have been able to reject him completely. His gentle smile of appreciation felt more like my undoing.

Thump, thump, thump. Not my heart, but Charli's tail striking the floor caught my attention. I became painfully aware that we were not alone and that Dad and Jewel were watching us with stupid grins on their faces as if we were Romeo and Juliet. I felt like reminding them what a disaster that coupling had been.

Charli behaved surprisingly willing to share my attentions. Of course, I never kiss him on the lips.

"Why don't we have some pie?" Jewel said at last, perhaps taking pity on me and my obvious discomfort.

Soon we were all seated at the table, and I thought, hoped, prayed that there would be no further excitement tonight.

So much for divine intervention.

Chapter Seven

I've never seen anyone flush as rapidly as Gary did. His eyes began swelling alarmingly. He shot me a look of panic.

"What kind of a pie did you say this was?" I asked, striding to the phone.

"Rhubarb, dear," she replied. With her hand on Gary's shoulder, she asked, "Are you all right?"

"Of course, he's not all right," Dad bellowed, standing over Gary as helplessly as she.

I called 911. "Were there strawberries in there?" I asked over the two of them arguing and Gary's breathing, which had become alarmingly labored.

"Strawberries?" Jewel asked, deducing the problem. I could tell by her tone of her voice that there had been.

"It's going to be all right, Gary. An ambulance is

on its way,'' I told him, kneeling beside him. ''He's horribly allergic to strawberries,'' I told Dad, who still seemed a bit puzzled.

''Oy, vey!'' Dad cried. ''You've killed him. Pie poisoning! If you hadn't been so preoccupied with what's his name, this never would have happened.''

''What?!'' Jewel answered over Gary's breathing and my shocked expression.

Dad started pacing. Our family resemblance proved uncanny. ''You're not yourself, Jewel. Ever since this John came into the picture, you just aren't thinking.''

''I'm not thinking?'' Jewel stood nose to nose with him. With the ambulance on its way, her nerves and exhaustion seemed to translate into a willingness to have a good brawl.

I stroked Gary's face, held my hand reassuringly to his back. He struggled to remain calm despite his very real distress. I was trying to think if I should run to the neighbor's house and see if they had any Benedryl when the Landview paramedics arrived. They assessed the patient and began treatment immediately. By the time we were about to leave for the hospital, Gary had already begun recovering from the IV drugs they had administered.

Grabbing my backpack, I followed the crew out the door. It was only then that I saw Charli sitting happily in Dad's chair, finishing off the rest of the strawberry-rhubarb pie.

Emergency rooms remind me of death. It doesn't matter how much corporate wallpaper and fresh flowers the places are decorated with. It doesn't matter how cutesy the staff's aqua scrub suits appear. It doesn't matter how spacious the nearly hotel room–size cubicles are. An emergency room makes me feel small and vulnerable. Forever nine years old, huddled on a chair in a corner, where someone had brought me because there weren't any special places for kids to wait while their mothers died. That long-ago day I'd had the worst and loneliest wait of my life, as I teetered between hope, which I was unaccustomed to, and futility, which had proved too constant a companion.

"Kathryn?" Jewel's voice penetrated my unwelcome lapse into recollection. I peered up into her compassionate face. She said nothing except my name, not needing to say any more. I knew that Gary would be fine. She knew what I had been thinking about. A glance around the cubicle revealed that Dad wasn't doing much better than I. Worse, actually. He had a look on his face that I hadn't seen in a while. It was a thirsty look, a desire for that one drink that would be too many and the million others that would never be enough.

I realized, to my embarrassment, that I'd been holding Gary's hand. At the moment, he seemed a good deal more composed than I. When my gaze met his, I discovered the kind of acceptance I had been starving for once upon a time and had assumed that I no longer needed. He knew what I was remembering. He knew about Dad's silent dilemma. On some fire-lit night long ago, I'd told him of the drunken truck driver, the collision, the sudden death of my mother.

"Are you feeling better?" I asked him, stretching for something to say.

"Much, thank you." He gave my hand a squeeze before allowing me to pull it free.

"Hymie?" Jewel said cautiously. "Gary's feeling much better now."

My father looked as though someone had spoken to him in Arabic and the meaning of their words had only just been translated. "Good. I'll be back."

"Hymie?" Jewel called as he swept out.

I felt my eyes glaze over with a veil of tears, which might hide, yet never extinguished, the fear that the man I'd come to love, accept, . . . and forgive would disappear, and the man who had caught and broken my mother's heart would return. I batted back those telltale tears.

It was Jewel's turn to look indecisive.

"Don't bother," I told her dryly, in the event that she harbored some intention of following him. "He'll either be back or he won't."

"Of course he'll be back," Jewel replied, worry furrowing her brow. "Of course he'll be back. . . ."

I closed my eyes against an ache, which threatened to stop my heart.

"Kathryn?"

Cole's voice somehow came as no surprise to me. This entire venture had taken on a dreamlike quality. Its surreal nature felt more pronounced while I mutely sat as Cole and Gary formally met. They were so comfortable with each other. So gentlemanly. It was all so civilized.

Suddenly, I felt everyone's attention on me.

"Her face is white as a sheet."

"Somebody get her some water."

"Put your head between your knees, sweetie," advised the bored nurse who had been tending Gary.

I did as she instructed. My forehead pounded. My skin felt clammy and chilled. *You will not lose your dignity*, I told myself privately. *Pull yourself together.*

After drawing several deep breaths, I sat upright and willed myself to not shake.

"Come on, Bogert," Cole said without a trace of emotion. "I need some coffee and you need to cough up the results of your prowling around, which I'm sure you've been doing."

Coffee sounded ghastly, but fleeing with an excuse had tremendous allure.

"Go on," Gary urged. "I'm sure they'll be done with me soon. You go with them, Ms. Johnson— Jewel. I'm really tired right now." As if to accentuate the point, he let his eyelids drift closed.

The three of us headed for the hospital cafeteria. It wasn't until we had arrived that I was truly feeling more like myself and able to notice that Jewel most definitely was not.

"Jewel?" I repeated for the third time. "Jewel?"

"Yes?" she answered absently.

"You have three different kinds of pie and a can of Coke on your tray," I pointed out.

"I do?" She surveyed the repast as though seeing it for the first time. "Silly me. I never drink Coke." Keeping the three slices of institutionally made pie, she put back the soda and replaced it with an iced tea.

At the cash register, Cole insisted on paying for everything. As Jewel wandered ahead, apparently in search of a place to sit, the detective whispered, "What's the matter with her?"

"Doesn't like hospitals," I answered nonchalantly, threading my way between the tables and chairs behind her. He didn't seem to believe me.

We took up residence in a booth near the window, where a magnificent display of hibiscus flourished. Their saffron heads were the size of cabbages, and I fancied they listed toward the window as though to eavesdrop on our conversation. At least Jewel seemed completely devoted to some sort of silent communion with them.

"So, Bogert," Cole said, taking a generous bite of poached salmon. Our hospital boasted better cuisine than half the restaurants in town. "Give. Where has your inquisitive little nose been today?"

"A better question," I replied, dragging a French fry through a pool of ketchup. "How did *you* just happen to be stopping by?" I pointed the fry at him. He leaned over and bit off the end.

"Heard the call come in," he said after finishing chewing. Hazarding a quick glance at Jewel, he added, "I was concerned it was about your father."

Jewel bit her lip but remained silent.

"I'm glad to know he's well. He is well, isn't he?" Cole continued.

That little query seemed to be enough for Jewel to cast off her concerns and rise to Hymie's defense. "Of course he's well. He probably had an errand. Remembered something that needed doing. I'm sure we'll catch up with him later. Isn't this salmon well prepared, detective?"

"Yes, ma'am."

"I remember when hospital food tasted like boiled cardboard." She went on with a tad too much joviality.

"One of your former students is probably the cook," I said, smiling.

"Oh, get on with you," she said, waving off the compliment. Apparently deciding to join us mentally and leave Hymie in the hands of a Higher Power, Jewel went on, "It's been pleasant teaching again. I'll be glad to see September, though, and get back to Jewel's full time. Teaching isn't what it used to be."

Cole continued eating, but I sensed his change in manner. It was rather like watching a chameleon gracefully shift color. "You used to teach with Gene Waite, didn't you?"

I cursed myself for not delving into this particular mine myself. It wouldn't be the first time that Jewel had produced vital information—without realizing it of course.

"Oh, yes," Jewel replied, shoving aside some barely tasted cherry pie. "Those days you had some authority. Pupils came to learn. Parents backed you up.

The kids may have had long hair, but most still retained their manners. This group . . . sometimes I feel like a cross between a prison guard and a babysitter.''

"Gene," I urged.

"Well, now. You ought to know, Kathryn. You were one of his pupils. Gene was one of those fellows with a gift for teaching. He didn't so much command respect as he made it almost a 'cool thing' to be allowed into his class."

A smile of remembrance softened my mouth. She'd said it perfectly. It had been a "cool thing" to be one of Gene's crowd: joking in the hall before class, screaming out answers as he generated nearly "Sesame Street" levels of energy, attending unofficial gatherings at the Pie Shoppe—where we shared stories and anecdotes and fears of the future. And now he was dead. What a waste.

"I don't know that any of us ended up rocket scientists," I said quietly, "but I believe that most of us at least tried to pursue a dream. Thanks to him. Thanks to his encouragement."

Cole remained silent. It was one of the things that I liked about him.

"What have you got, Kathryn?" he said at last.

"You first," I replied, lifting an eyebrow.

He leaned his long body back in his chair. Carefully wiping his mouth with his napkin, he popped a toothpick between his teeth for munching and said, "You've got to be kidding."

Fidgeting a little, I said, "Worth a try, you know. Can't fault a girl for trying."

A dark expression passed over him. He chewed that toothpick until it snapped.

"Look, you . . ." He seemed unable to find the perfect term or expletive. "How's this for first? The gun Charli found under the ping-pong table is hot. It was traced to a robbery in Pulaski. A robbery where the clerk was shot and killed. Now are you ready to talk to me?"

Chapter Eight

Homicide? The idea of Gene being involved on any level in an armed robbery was ludicrous. I didn't have to rise to his defense.

"Surely, you don't believe that Gene had anything to do with such a crime," Jewel exclaimed, as though affronted for all retired teachers everywhere. She gripped her fork in her fist.

Cole's silence served as his reply. Meanwhile, my mind was leapfrogging to alternate possibilities with the desperation of someone struggling for their last glimpse of sunlight. It was a "frame." Someone—or, for that matter, more than one individual—wanted Gene to take responsibility for their crime. A person or persons unknown had crept into his house and stowed the gun . . .

. . . Gene had come into possession of the gun accidentally and until he could decide what to do with it, he'd hidden it under the table.

Ballistics had made a mistake! That was it. Some technician had had too many Margaritas at happy hour. . . . The technician had been paid off!

All of these scenarios, ranging from the possible to the ridiculous, flickered through my mind like the final gasp of dying match.

I felt compelled to meet Cole's steady gaze. Somewhere in the cafeteria, a man laughed intrusively long and hard. Beside us a sprinkler began flinging water in a liquid cadence against the window.

Finding the gun hidden the way that it was looked bad. It looked very bad for Gene Waite. If the detective doubted Gene's involvement in the robbery, I knew professionalism would prevent him from declaring that fact. Nevertheless, this fresh crime lent a new, increasingly dangerous slant to the police investigation. The circumstances of Gene's hit-and-run were becoming even more confusing the further we delved. I couldn't help wondering about the dead store clerk. Had it been a student? An immigrant? A woman working nights to provide food money for her kids? I didn't ask. Somehow I feared that the answer might keep me awake nights.

The second bedroom, which I'd converted into my art studio, nearly called my name as I tried to slip past it down the hall.

''Shoot,'' I said, stopping outside the door.

Vignettes passed through my mind. Faces. More

than faces. Bold, revealing portraits with nearly abstract components. Portraits *my way*. I'd yet to begin the work that had been my companion for so long. After my former client, Gertrude Trent, had virtually disappeared for parts unknown, leaving only a succession of international postcards as clues to her whereabouts, I'd yearned to begin *Gertrude*.

The series of paintings that I envisioned were too revealing to be simple flattery. Their honesty, their emotion, their drive, I hope, would render them nearly mystical and yet entirely of this earth.

Charli yawned near my feet.

I glanced down. The dog appeared ready to fall asleep sitting up. He swayed a bit, with his eyes closed.

Paint me, the voice of my soul whispered. My evening's nap had left me more awake than not, particularly under the circumstances.

"Circumstances," I told myself, shoving away something I didn't wish to look at. Something much older and possibly more intimidating than my brush. So saying, I pressed past Charli, and flicked on several lights. The dog ambled over to the day bed near the wall, leaped onto it, dug, dug, dug, turned, and flopped. Peering at me out of one eye, he seemed to wait permission to sleep.

I walked over, tousled his fur, and planted a kiss—not on the lips, mind you—on the top of his head. "Good night, Charli," I told him.

He groaned and relaxed as only an animal in repose can do. Stripping felt as though I were shedding my skin. I went into the adjacent bathroom, brushed my teeth, and donned some work/sleep clothes. (They frequently turned out to be one and the same thing.)

After curling up in the battered recliner beside Charli, I adjusted a halogen lamp to shine over my sketch pad and several photos that I'd thought to work with. With my feet curled beneath me and my flannel shirt tucked around me, I studied the pad.

For a moment, I saw Gary on the pristine white. Flushed and desperate. Then, as he had looked after he'd kissed me, virile and appreciative. The warmth in my gut turned to fire as the image changed. My father. Leaving us. Never returning.

I nearly broke the charcoal pencil in my hand. I squeezed it so hard. With determination, I drew to mind the image that had first suggested this series. A former client, Gertrude Trent, no invalid she, her head supported by the tired magenta of the wing chair, which she sat upon as though it were a throne. Her arresting eyes. The prominent nose. And behind that keenly intelligent face, the under washing of chronic pain that seemed her birthright. An image beyond determination, short of resignation. Life. In that moment.

My hand began moving across the paper. Bit by bit, what I wanted to paint returned in my mind. It loomed and grew to obliterate everything else—my doubts, my fears, Gene's death. Breathing it in, I slipped out of myself and my life and existed as nothing but a force wielding a pencil.

*   *   *

Footsteps on the stairs finally gripped my attention.

He'd managed to creep into the house and reach halfway to the second floor before some second sense of mine broke through my trancelike state. I paused, staring ahead into the yawning emptiness of the open doorway.

No telltale stumble. No slurred mumbling.

I waited.

He came to the top of the stairs and I knew that the light glowing from my room would generally bring him creeping by. To smile affectionately. Watch indulgently. Tap his watch, as a reminder that even artists must sleep some time.

A lifetime of memories might have swirled through the void of silence, which characterized his indecision. As I heard him turn and move in the opposite direction toward his room, I felt part of my soul tumble and pinwheel like autumn leaves in his wake, heralding a winter that could prove our last.

It took a moment for my focus to return to my work, but it did. There was nothing. Nothing except "Gertrude" and me and the force that bound us inexorably together.

I must have slept deeply, for I've no recollection of the time passing. When I awoke, Charli was gone and the bits of sunlight that had escaped a grey day could have suggested early morning or late afternoon. From the dryness of my mouth and the groggy feeling in my head, I decided my Frosted Flakes were probably hours overdue.

Flopping over onto my stomach, I let the warmth of the mattress seep into my belly. On the floor beside me lay the sketches I'd executed last night. Contentment stroked back other concerns. Yes. I could do this. The colors were in my mind. The textures. And the image. It was here, right here on this pad.

Cheerfully, I strode to the bathroom to take care of my morning requirements. As shower water sluiced blessedly over my weary muscles, I contemplated the day. No point in going to the Waites', or at least not until later. Cole would probably have it off-limits to me. I could use the time to check out the Melody Joy gallery, I considered as I dried off.

All this and more traipsed merrily across my mental schedule. When I arrived downstairs and saw the Oktoberfest still in residence, it felt like I'd inhaled cold mud. The reality of last night grew vivid. I was beyond caring for my father's explanations or excuses. The very fact that I'd had to even consider possibilities felt unacceptable.

Suddenly, I knew exactly how I was going to spend the day. It took less than five minutes to make the arrangements over the telephone.

Then I sat down to eat my Frosted Flakes.

Sue ''Sells'' Selton offered to drive us and I didn't have the heart to refuse her. She pulled into the driveway behind the wheel of a new bright-orange Volkswagen sporting her SUE ''SELLS'' SELTON signs. I was reminded of some nursery rhyme pumpkin house, except this one had wheels.

Charli approached the vehicle warily.

"I think he's wondering if it's edible," I told Sue dryly.

"Of course it's not edible," she replied in her perkiest cheerleader-to-the-world voice. "Here, Charli," she said, leaning over. "I had this made up just for you."

Before she could attach the bright-orange collar lettered SUE "SELLS" SELTON, I gently yet determinedly caught her wrist. "That's awfully sweet of you. We'll pass."

She withdrew her hand and gave me a smile, which nearly concealed the shrewd business woman she was behind all that innocence. "Just keep it." She scrunched her nose and plunked the collar into my hand.

Charli leapt into the backseat as I sat shotgun. Sue checked her flawless reflection in the rearview mirror as she began, "Believe it or not, I knew you'd be calling one of these days. Actually had a file on you just in case."

The super Realtor of Landview no doubt had files to rival J. Edgar Hoover's. Anything if it could lead to a sale.

"I know that your last place was by the river— really a terrible thing about that fire, what ever happened to that arsonist?—and as you know property over there is hard to find. . . ."

I let the breeze from the open window wash over me as she spoke. The further we drove from the Sears home, the lighter my heart felt, and the more determined I became to move on. I missed half of what Sue was saying, since I didn't really care. When I saw the place that was right for me, I'd know it.

". . . Anyway." Her change of tone and the slowing of the car caught my attention. "I thought you might want to consider a change of venue," Sue finished as she cut the engine.

She'd left us at the end of a long stone driveway. The driveway and the house at the end of it seemed buttressed by forest on all sides. Except for a free-for-all lawn, trees and shrubs jumbled and burst and thrust skyward in more shades of green than I could imagine. Caterpillar, grass, malachite, hunter, emerald. The air proved redolent of forest, moist and fresh as though the trees had been caught exhaling. It seemed blessedly hushed.

Sue remained silent. So did Charli.

I stepped out of the car almost reverently. Somehow, someway, someone had designed a modest house in the style of Frank Lloyd Wright here in good ol' Landview. The lines and expanses of wood and windows blended with and accented the surroundings. I could imagine the sort of light that might spill into my studio inside.

Letting my backpack slip to the ground beside a cluster of saffron jonquils, I began moseying to the right to glimpse the property from different angles. Meanwhile, Charli bounded out of the car and proceeded to hustle up to the front door and back before he realized that there were squirrels in them there woods. He was off.

"How many bedrooms?" I asked striving for non-chalance. She probably knew she'd sold the place, but then one must go through the motions. No matter what it was like inside, I could have it renovated. This property was a lesson in Location, Location, Location.

"Three good-sized," Sue replied, checking her listing. "An eat-in kitchen, dining room, stone fireplace, added redwood deck in the back, thermopane windows, furnace . . ."

I let her give me the rundown as I walked toward the front door, a carved oak affair with a brass knocker shaped like—Emmet the Clown? Ah, well. Gaining the front porch, I sensed the embrace of the overhang, the invitation of that silly clown. I loved it.

An indoor tour proved nearly unnecessary. It was everything I had imagined and more. The only modification that I foresaw that might require immediate attention was the installation of a skylight in one of the bedrooms, which I would use as my studio. As I contemplated the peace and serenity of the place, the quiet was shattered by canine ruckus.

Charli had gone into full-bark mode. Guess he'd already gotten a bit proprietary. Either that or someone was trying to steal Sue's Volks.

"We'd better see what's bothering him," I said. Sue nodded abstractly. She was working on a laptop at the kitchen counter, trying to pull together some figures for me and no doubt hoping to cinch the deal. Leaving her to her labors, I trailed Charli's noise to the front door. I arrived in time to see him capering and barking at something just past Sue's car. As I stepped outside, he bolted toward the back, where the driveway continued on past the house to a small, free-standing garage.

"Charli!" I called. Visions of skunks and tomato-juice baths had begun filling my mind. Ticks and fleas and Lyme disease . . . Maybe this wasn't the house for us.

"Charli!"

A blue Escort had pulled up in front of our garage. The engine still ran. I could barely make out the two figures in the car. To my horror, Charli began clawing at the driver's-side door, whining and mewing. Striding over quickly, I figured that any minute the driver would emerge with a baseball bat and kill my dog. Forget skunks. Perhaps this secluded location harbored more dangerous wildlife.

"Get down!" I yelled. "Charli!"

It wasn't until I'd gotten within spitting distance that I glimpsed the driver's shoulder holster. Forget the baseball bat. Whoever was in the car was toting a gun.

Chapter Nine

Shock and fear may be two entirely different reactions, but they can create very similar biological responses. As the driver emerged from the car, I found myself rooted in disbelief, confusion, and possibly horror. Vital signs: accelerated pulse, cold and clammy skin, slight vertigo.

"Okay, Bogert," Phil said, easing her shoulders beneath her Cubs jacket. "What gives?"

My eyes narrowed. What gives indeed? I was about to point out that she was trespassing on my soon-to-be-acquired property when I noticed something disturbing. What I had originally taken to be a garage was, in fact, a small house tucked right up against the boundary of the woods. Oh no. I knew this was too good to be true. Drug dealers, prostitutes, criminal elements had found my dream property. Was I sharing it? Was this actually two separate lots? Had I stumbled upon the "Twilight Zoning?"

Not one to unnecessarily give away any info, I patted Charli to quiet him down and returned her question. "What gives with you? Working a case?"

"Gah!" a voice called from inside the car. Peering through the window, I caught the bright gaze of little Dot Matrix. Dot had acquired her unusual name and her mixed heritage from a mother and father who were too strung out and immature to be parents. Sometimes I wondered how Phil would take it if her sister ever did return to claim the child. Dot was seated in a toddler seat shaped like a stuffed Dalmatian. Her pudgy hands reached for me opening and closing. Past experience had taught me that she was as capable of pulling my hair out by the roots as of hugging me.

"Hi'ya, Dot," I said cheerfully. Charli made his way around to the kid's side of the car to entertain her. I couldn't help wondering where Tommy Panozzo, the pizza king, was. Generally, while Phil worked, he tended the baby.

I had begun to feel more curious than alarmed, as I believed that Phil wouldn't knowingly bring Dot into a dangerous situation under any circumstances.

For a fraction of a second I thought I detected something vulnerable in the detective.

"At least my work serves some purpose," she snapped. "You ever going to get a life, instead of lapping up the remnants of other people's?"

So much for vulnerable.

"Actually," I replied, feeling magnanimous due to my sudden windfall, "I was . . ."

Not to finish my sentence. A huge, honkin' four-wheeler crunched past Sue's Bug and ate the gravel approaching us. Various stickers hawked messages on the front bumper, which caught my attention.

Maybe this was a drug bust, I considered, as a bear of a man ambled out of the car followed by his hillbilly facsimile on the other side. I felt my "snob talons" extending. Such a trying character defect.

"Hey there, Miz Panozzo," he said, extending his burly hand toward Phil.

"Detective," she gritted through her teeth.

"Detective?" The guy shot his wife an unreadable glance. "Is that so? Now you didn't mention that when we wuz discussin' leases an' all."

Leases? Phil definitely appeared uncomfortable now.

The pear-shaped woman peeled the wrapper off a candy bar as though it were a banana and took a huge bite. After wiping her hand on her jeans with marginal effectiveness, she spoke around a mouthful of chocolate. "Don't mind him, honey," she said to Phil. "He just gets a little prickly around the cops. The family used to get arrested quite regular."

Phil pulled her hand back with a pained expression. As much as she tried to ignore me, I could sense her desire for my departure.

"Why don't you scratch for earthworms somewhere else, Bogert?" she said, indicating with a tip of her head that I should leave.

"Scratch for earthworms. Hah. There's a funny," the man said, laughing and slapping his thigh, which brought on a coughing fit. He hacked and hacked and brought up something nearly the size of a fur ball. Very attractive.

The phlegm must have contained his sense of humor. Not too kindly he went on. "Now, I thought you said it was jest you and the little one. We gotta be careful with codes and all. N' other thing. I wouldn't be wantin' no pets. Mess up the property values."

Charli looked affronted. Phil maintained her cool, yet I perceived a slight pallor beneath her expression, which never manifested itself in work situations and rarely did so in private ones.

Glancing back at the house, I noticed Sue emerging from the back door onto the deck. Phil misses nothing. The realtor's appearance could not have escaped her notice. Did her complexion shift from white to grey?

The pregnant pause was shattered by Garth Brooks. Not in person. An ancient van, which looked as though it were coated with zinc oxide, swung in the drive, wove perilously past the Bug, and careened to a halt behind the four-wheeler.

One, two, three, four, five, six persons, aged early teens to late twenties, tumbled out the side door to the strains of "Stand by Your Man."

"Yo, man," the driver said in a voice a step ahead of laryngitis. "This be one cool crib. Is that the house you was tellin' us about, Uncle Zach?" He pointed with his bottle hand toward "my garage." Fortunately for him, he was only toting a Coke.

"Heck, no," the woman said, snatching the youngest of the brood into an unwelcome hug. "It's that one."

To my horror, she pointed to the perfect deck of my dream house. Now it was my turn to panic. Sue, obviously sensing a glitch in her plans, breezed down the steps and hastened toward us. The males in the new contingent stood agog at her deliberate approach.

"May I help you?" Sue asked with the cut of a paring knife.

A consultation/confrontation ensued that I thought not to intrude upon. Instead, I turned to Phil. She seemed to have similar inclinations.

"You . . . and Tommy thinking about a move?" I asked carefully. Their oversized, overpriced two-story had never seemed to Phil's liking. It had always been my impression that it spoke of her husband's pretensions more than her tastes.

"Don't be coy, Bogert," she said, an edge of weariness in her voice. "You heard the man. He didn't mention anything about Tommy."

For a moment, I didn't think she would either. Then Charli—who has an incredible sense of empathy, if you want my opinion—came curling around her legs. She languidly stroked his head. "Tommy," Phil volunteered, "decided that he'd like a change of scene. So he left the restaurant—and me—and took off. Don't worry, he brought the neighborhood Lolita along to keep him company."

"We wouldn't want him to be lonely, now would we?" I replied catlike. My feminist muscles were flexing and my loyalty factor to my oldest nemesis made it easy to really detest the guy whom I'd never thought much of to begin with.

"Not a bit," Phil answered nonchalantly. She cast a glance over my shoulder, where Sue and Uncle Zach were continuing their animated "discussion" about purchase prerogatives. The crew from the van had set up on the lawn in a loose circle. They were enjoying a picnic lunch from some fast-food restaurant. Charli scavenged for rejected slices of pickle. He can be so plebeian.

"Nice place, isn't it?" I said, gesturing at the surrounding woods.

"Yeah," Phil replied, leaning into the car to unfasten Dot, who had been still long enough.

The little girl clung to the lapel of the detective's jacket with one hand and sucked her thumb with her other, and I knew that this was just the pose I wanted to capture for the next painting. Cop. Mother. Friend. Did I say friend?

"Don't worry, Bogert," she said, interrupting my flight of fancy. "I'll find other digs."

The woman who was not squared off against Sue overheard her.

"No, you won't, honey. You signed a lease. Six months. Already cashed your security deposit, didn't I, Zach? Zach?"

Zach turned away from Sue. His face was broken out in a sweat. His complexion florid. Sue hadn't mussed a hair.

"That's right. Buyin' that weird house is one thing. Rentin' this one is another."

My eyes narrowed. He called my house "weird."

"Excuse me," I said, stepping into the fray. "But that house is no longer for sale."

Sue beamed.

"I just bought it," I added.

The burger contingent erupted in hoots and hollers. Zach and his woman squared off for a scream fest. Sue had whipped out a cellular phone. I caught Phil's eye over all of it. Apparently, Detective Panozzo and I were going to become neighbors.

As we drove back toward town, I confess to being in a somewhat dazed condition. Charli smelled of fresh onion and pickle. Sue chattered away. I entertained unpleasant visions of waking up in the morning to see Phil coming in from a midnight shift. I groaned.

What could I do? I loved the house. And the rental would be a great place to raise a kid. I couldn't very well leave Dot in the neighborhood with Zach's extended family for neighbors. And, all right, I couldn't walk away from Phil either. She was a pain in the . . . posterior. But I suppose she was my friend, in a peculiar sort of way. I wondered—not for the first time—where our relationship would be had I not blocked her perfect spike during the final game of the volleyball tournament our senior year in high school. She'd never forgiven me the loss of that winning point.

"You've made the right decision," Sue was saying. "That property really is a steal. The land on three sides is forest preserve, so you won't have to worry about developers.''

''Where are we going?'' I asked, realizing that Sue was probably hastening to her office to secure my John Hancock as soon as possible.

''I thought it would be convenient to swing by the office to sign the papers before I take you home,'' Sue confirmed, beaming. ''I'm sure you can pre-qualify for a loan.''

''Yeah, sure,'' I answered dully. Buyers' remorse can hit you with the severity and suddenness of the Asian flu. On the bright side, I reassured myself that the semi-secluded location of the house would be conducive to artistic excellence. Then, as we traversed into an even more isolated area, my mind moved to other topics. Suddenly, a modicum of curiosity breached my ennui. There was something about this road. Where were we?

''Stop the car,'' I ordered.

''What?''

''Stop the car.'' I'm not sure if she thought I was about to be ill or not, but Sue complied.

Seventy-five yards ahead I had glimpsed the weathered wooden bridge, which arched above Land's Creek. It wasn't the creek, nor the particular density of the oaks and bushes in the surrounding woods, that caught my attention. It was the congregation of fifteen or so teenagers who had clustered off the shoulder of the road—some carrying bouquets, others holding wreaths or single blossoms.

I stepped out of the car. Charli padded behind me.

As I closed the distance between myself and the group, the grinding of the pebbled shoulder beneath my feet offered scant stability. I felt keenly aware of the narrow nature of the roadway and the absence of any form of street light, electrical wiring, or road signs that might have made the spot more welcoming. Ebony flashes, which might have been sun spots, led me closer. My thoughts drifted to a certain night. Had there been moonlight to illumine the area? Would the evening temperature have necessitated a spring jacket?

Gene I thought, *what would have brought you to this lonely place and such a tragic end?*

A sledgehammer of a man at the head of the group took notice of me. The teenagers turned in my direction, offering mournful faces, that had been newly initiated into grief.

"May I help you?" the fellow asked in a high voice totally at odds with his frame.

"I'd like to join you if I might?" I answered, reaching the fringes of the crowd.

He nodded sullenly and returned to his litany. I didn't hear the words. The tears choking me seemed to block my other senses. In so many ways, Gene had been a father to me when my own dad had been preoccupied with Jim Beam. I wished I'd have spent more time with him. I wished I could tell him what he meant to me. I wished all the things a person wishes when a sudden death claims a cherished relative or friend.

The students—I'd learned this was Gene's current brood—were laying their memorial when I heard Sue's voice beside me.

"This is where it happened, wasn't it?" she asked with empathy.

The sort of question that required no answer.

"I'm sorry, Kathryn. I didn't realize. He was your teacher, too, wasn't he?"

I nodded past the lump in my throat and swallowed with effort. Grief gave way to determination. Whatever happened on this road, I was going to ferret it out. Whoever killed Gene would not go anonymously on as though he or she had done no more than strike a wayward rabbit. Manslaughter or murder, I would find out the truth.

"Come on, Charli," I said, snapping my fingers. I left the mourners and started over to the bridge, examining the ground and surroundings for anything that might help. Certainly the police had collected evidence, but that wasn't my specialty. I collected ideas, fantasies. I'd the ability to imagine a scene and what might have led up to it.

"Kathryn," Sue said with less compassion than before. "Don't you think we ought to be going?" She plucked her orange high heel out of the muck that she'd stepped in trying to tail me.

The bridge was a landmark on this unremarkable road, a place where a meeting might have taken place. Or Gene might have stopped here merely because he'd swerved to avoid one of the deer that occasionally bounded across the road. Somehow his car had ended up on the shoulder of the road unblemished and he had ended up in the street fatally wounded.

"Kathryn? You really should leave this to the authorities. We could be back at the office in twenty minutes. If we dawdle, someone else might just get a bid in before us.''

I stopped dead in my tracks, turned, and stared at her. She had the grace to blush.

Brushing a ladybug off her orange suit jacket lapel, Sue sighed. ''Tacky. I agree. What can I do to help you? What are we looking for?''

Filling her in on what I knew so far and all I didn't know, we navigated the woods on both sides of the road. When I didn't say anything about the gun or the robbery, when I neglected to mention that Gene had acquired stolen goods, I had to face the fact that there was one question I didn't want to consider. Was Gene Waite the man I thought he was? What if he had been involved in criminal activity and had not been just an innocent?

Our search of the area proved silent due to these sudden reflections.

''Okay,'' Sue said after a while, sitting down on a stump and brushing her blonde hair back with her wrist. Perspiration had begun glistening her face. She swatted at a swarm of gnats haloing her head. ''Since Gene didn't run out of gas, and his car didn't break down, my guess would be that he was meeting someone here.''

I grasped the railing of the bridge and leaned forward to study the murky water meandering below through dead leaves, blackened sticks, and tentacled tree roots. A rustling of undergrowth suggested the rapid flight of a small animal. The water moved silently for the most part, except where it picked up speed around a jutting collection of concrete bricks someone had dumped into the creek. *The meeting could have had something to do with the missing fourth edition*, I considered glumly.

"It was around midnight." I tossed a stick into the water and watched it pinwheel out of sight. "He wasn't much of a night owl. In order for him to agree to meet someone at that time of night, he must have known them pretty well. . . ."

". . . And had a good reason," Sue said, her face a portrait of concentration. I doubted if she had allowed herself to be this oblivious to her physical appearance since kindergarten. I found myself liking her better a little dirty.

"Family?" I offered.

"Business?" she said shrewdly.

"Why not both?" I conjectured, turning and facing Sue. "Lizzie was pretty eager to pin a murder on her mother. What if she killed her father?"

Instead of appearing shocked, Sue looked as though she'd just bitten a juicy apple.

"What about the wife? Maybe she wanted a little more out of life? Maybe wanted him to retire and move with her to Tampa and he wouldn't. Maybe she wanted to sell the house and go condo and he wouldn't. What if she were secretly planning to divorce him and decided to go for the insurance money instead?"

Before Sue could write an entire screenplay, I held my hand up. "Motive, means, and opportunity," I said as though I really knew what I was talking about. Her face skewed in concentration. "My understanding is that Mary made or had plenty of money on her own.

"Come on, Sue," I added lightheartedly. "Why don't we head back to your office and transact some business? I appreciate your support, but I think I need to let some of this sink in before I leap to any conclusions."

"All right." She stood and eased her shoe back on as she'd been rubbing her stockinged foot.

In no time, Sue "Sells" Selton was back on Realtor track. She went on and on about the sterling qualities of "my" house as we approached the outskirts of Landview.

"Now that guy," Sue said, gesturing with her head to yet another ceremony being enacted on this bright afternoon, "I don't trust at all."

Since we'd been halted by a near-comatose freight train, I had the opportunity to study the object of Sue's disdain. Before I could place him, Sue continued. "Mr. Park Commissioner claims that he wants to annex forest for a new park. Not likely. I can smell political aspirations, and he's got them. More than that, he has the feel of a shark. Businesswise."

She offered a toothy smile. "Takes one to know one," she confessed.

It was that person from Preston's who had tried to jump the Fuzzy Wuzzy line. Cutting the ribbon on what was obviously a dedication ceremony for a piece of playground equipment was the whiner, his daughter. The child watched her father's speech with what could only be described as a sly expression.

"What's his name?" I asked.

"Dick Chase," Sue answered, "a manufacturer. He owns that dish factory by the expressway."

I studied him for a moment. If he was a joker, then he had the role of citizen-of-the-year down real well.

All of a sudden, Sue made a noise like a cat being strangled. She'd caught a glimpse of herself in the rearview mirror. Her hand rose and she reached to the bits of dead leaf dotting her coiffure. She swiped frantically at a brush of dirt on her cheek. Some folks just aren't used to mucking around in the woods. I swung my arm around her shoulder and leaned my equally wind-blown head against hers. We caught each other's smile in the mirror.

"You really are a menace, Kathryn Bogert," she said, shaking her head.

"Likewise, I'm sure."

Charli simply barked.

Chapter Ten

A sense of guilt proved an unwelcome companion when Sue deposited me at Dad's house. His Saturn was parked in the drive and I supposed he'd closed up the barbershop early to come home and prepare his let's-make-amends dinner. I wasn't sure I felt ready to tackle last night or the future, so I dawdled outside. So much had happened in that house. I'd grown. I'd left. I'd returned. And now I would leave again. My heart felt reassuringly lighter at the thought.

Cole would never have caught me unawares had I not been mooning around about my new adventure.

"Have you got a few minutes?" he asked.

Although I was inclined to say no, I'd little interest in doing the "we can talk at the station routine." Also, any excuse to avoid going inside held tremendous appeal. This was three times in so many days that Cole had sort of "popped up." Surprisingly, I wasn't exactly displeased.

When I didn't invite him in, the detective surely noticed but made no remark. Instead, he suggested that I join him for a cup of coffee. I negotiated for a cola slush and the three of us headed over to the new Super Kmart.

As I reveled in my personal drug of choice, Cole shook his head, saying, "I'd rather drink the winter drippings off snow tires."

I noisily drained my glass. "I'll take another hit," I told him, gesturing at the serving bar with my straw.

"Just a minute," he replied. As he walked away, I considered what a good guy he was. He didn't have to buy me cola slushes. Why was he buying me cola slushes anyway?

He returned and planted my second cola slush on the table in front of me. Those grey eyes gave nothing away. I toyed with the concoction in front of me. Finally, I broke the silence first.

"So," I said, looking off at a point beyond his shoulder. "Have you made any progress?"

To my surprise, he actually answered me.

"Do you know a Brad Paladin?" Cole rolled a bit of straw between his fingers. I noticed that he'd seemed to have the move from toothpick and coffee-stirrer crunching, i.e., oral fixation, to the less noticeable manual fidget. The nicotine fiend is one tough adversary.

Brad Paladin? The name sounded vaguely familiar

as only a couple of notes might from a long forgotten melody.

I shook my head no and took a long pull of slush. I loved the way the cold sort of shot through my sinuses and bolted into a bursting black balloon behind my eyes. Ah, well.

"It's the license number that you gave me. That '87 Pinto. Belongs to a guy named Brad Paladin," Cole said, leaning back against the comfortless red plastic booth. A saccharine voice over an intercom announced a special on jackets in the men's department.

"Connections?" I asked.

He lifted an eyebrow at me and might have smothered a smile. "Alumni of LHS." He offered a graduation year that was several behind mine.

Suddenly, those isolated notes coalesced into a refrain. "I didn't know him, but Gene did. I'm sure of it. I remember him telling me once about this guy who really had a great novel in him but couldn't seem to get it together." Eagerly, I shoved my slush aside and leaned forward. Charlie tried to reposition himself under the table. I could feel him smashed between my legs and the table's. "Does he have a record? Did you find anything else?"

"Not really. See what you can find out about him, why don't you?" Cole replied, so offhandedly that I believe he thought I might not have registered the significance of his request.

"Whoa!" I cried, reaching forward to grasp his hand. "Did I just hear you ask me for help? Information? Mr. Stay-out-of-my-investigation-or-else?"

He yanked his hand back and sort of growled. "I did not. I . . . oh, forget it."

There was something slightly petulant and cute about gruff old "King Cole" caught dropping his solo act. I decided not to tease him further. Besides, this was probably the closest I would get to honorary detective in my entire life. I wondered what could have motivated him to such an unusual position.

"Do you think he might have been too shy," I asked, "to attend the funeral and the wake?"

"That would explain one incident, but not the other. Why was he following you at Sweet Woods?"

"Well," I replied, deciding I'd had enough of K-mart. I stood and walked over to deposit my cup in the trash receptacle. Cole accompanied me, pausing to request a coffee refill. "Maybe he just happened to be there."

The detective paused, putting a lid on his cup. He held my gaze. "Maybe," he replied. I didn't get the impression that he meant it.

With coffee time over, I had little choice except to return to the old homestead. I felt hungry. That helped motivate me. Besides, I was eager to get to a pencil and paper. Anytime I'm trying to solve a mystery, I simply have to use visual aids. I need to make charts, diagrams, simple pictures. It helps me visualize the fuller picture.

As I stood with my hand on the front-door knob, the impact of the day's decisions hit me. My reasons for moving out forced their way past other thoughts.

Charli bounded past me at the front door into the kitchen. I heard my father greet him.

"Hey there, boy. How's my boy today? Did you have a good day? Did you? Are you hungry?"

Noises of Dad rustling up dog chow followed. I entertained a pang of guilt that Charli would be moving out with me. After all, Dad loved the dog. He loved both of us, I guess.

"Katie?" Dad was the only one who got away with calling me that. "Katie?"

"Yes, Dad."

"Dinner will be ready in about ten minutes. I made you a nice pot roast."

"Thanks. I'll be down after I wash up."

At the door of my bedroom, I paused to absorb my surroundings. The "no-hope" chest that had been left to me by my mother. She'd told me to fill it with dreams for when I'd lost all hope. It was one of my few keepsakes. The ceiling, which was shot with faded glow-in-the-dark galaxy stickers. I would wing my way through those stars on the darkest of nights. The desk of my childhood groaned under the burden of my computer/home office. I had to leave. I couldn't play the game anymore. I couldn't pretend that the past had never happened or that fear of its return didn't haunt me.

I retired to the washroom to clean up.

"The pot roast is very good," I observed shortly.

"Thank you."

Awkward pause.

"More potatoes?" he asked.

"Please."

In the background, the hum of the refrigerator motor seemed oppressively noisy. Charli had apparently absorbed the mood of the room and performed none of his usual jockeying for crumbs. As I sat mutely across from Dad, I felt a hollow sensation that prevented me from experiencing anger, hurt, or fear of domination. Not sure how to tell my father my big news, I decided to broach a less volatile subject. We could talk about the case. Solving other people's tragedies is, always, so much easier than acknowledging our own.

"Did I tell you that Cole traced that license plate number?"

Dad looked up. Shoving his plate to the side, he almost smiled. "Ah, Katie. And I suppose he wouldn't tell you what he learned, eh?"

"Actually, he did," I replied, tasting the meal for the first time. "I'm afraid I've got more questions now than ever."

As though he read my mind, Dad fetched a pad of paper, which we used to make grocery lists on. I tore off the top sheet to expose the blank white of the paper below, saying, "Let's play Hollywood Squares."

I drew a hefty grid that consisted of three spaces across and three spaces below.

Dad pointed at the first corner. "Put the guy in the car there, Katie."

I printed "Brad Paladin." While I sketched in what I knew about him, I told Dad, "We have to think expansively. Remember."

Second space. "How about that Gladys Zimmerman?" my father suggested. "That lady is a piece of work. To besmirch a man's shiva with her conniving ways. There's a name for ladies like her and it's not 'lady.' "

"Basically," I told Dad, sketching what I thought was a pretty decent caricature of Gladys, "while the other folks at the flea market want justice, she'd like me to find whatever windfall Gene may have come into, and turn it over to her."

"Terrible," Dad said.

"She believes it's a rare collection of Fuzzy Wuzzies. The fourth edition." I filled Dad in on the peculiar history of the Fuzzies and their potential worth.

"You know, if he made some kind of clandestine meeting to pick up a shipment of these things . . . maybe that was what he was doing the night he was killed." Dad's eyes gleamed with speculation.

"Nope. Gladys said that this was a few weeks before he was killed."

The doorbell rang, precluding further discussion. Yep. Seven o'clock. Precisely. Apparently after last night's reception, Jewel had elected to be completely punctual. When I met her at the door, her "hello" seemed a bit forced. I took the cake carrier from her and deduced by its weight that she had somehow taken the time to prepare Dad's favorite—pineapple upside down cake.

"Is he in the kitchen?" she asked softly.

"He's right here, my darling Jewel. Don't you look lovely tonight? What's this? Is she holding what I think she's holding?'' He reached for the cake and beamed a bit too merrily. Jewel melted beneath his admiration and the jaded part of me felt sorry for her. ''My favorite. My favorite cake from my favorite girl. My two favorite girls.''

My earlier resentment returned. I ducked back into the kitchen without a remark.

''So,'' Jewel said nervously as she watched Dad prepare the table for dessert. ''Looks like we're working on something.''

I had just finished writing ''Lizzie Waite'' in the third corner of the diagram.

''A suspect party. How jolly!'' she cried.

Dad had grown sullen, as though he'd finally noticed my change in mood.

I gripped my pencil. She wasn't going to ask him where he'd been last night. She was going to pretend nothing had happened. He was too. I suppose what really aggravated me wasn't their behavior, but my own. I hadn't confronted my father either. He sat at the table waiting for his cake, displaying an unnerving combination of preoccupation and patience.

''Lizzie could have all the classic motives for eliminating her father,'' Jewel said while she cut the cake. ''*Maybe* the Fuzzy Wuzzy thing is a red herring.''

Dad had begun toying with his knife. Maybe he was going to offer an explanation for last night after all.

''I don't know,'' I said, trying to ignore Dad and answer Jewel. Suddenly, Fuzzy Wuzzies seemed to appear in every square. Gladys. Phil. Dick Chase. The teaser left on my front porch. No. The Fuzzy Wuzzies were involved. Where a gun and armed robbery came in I had no idea. "Maybe I'd better try and get into the Waites' basement and see if I can find the box of Fuzzies that our merry window thought was missing. I hadn't paid much attention to it at the time, but . . ."

Out of the corner of my eye, I detected Dad opening and closing his fists. What was his problem anyway?

I sketched in Mary Waite's name and Victor Stempniak's. "She's not exactly the picture of grief," I remarked. "I could snoop around a little and find out more about their marriage. Maybe there's more to her relationship with her 'associate' than business. Maybe—"

Finishing my statement proved impossible. My father shoved himself noisily away from the table. Standing, his face twisted with hostility, he said, "Why don't you leave her alone? What's wrong with you anyway?!"

That did it. "What's wrong with me?" I stood and stared daggers at him from my side of the table. My irritation rose like a geyser and erupted with equal ferocity. "You're the one who is driving Jewel out of your life with your childish jealousy. You're the one who left us flat in the ER last night. Where did you go, Dad? Have an emergency meeting with a jigger?" I cried, shocking myself as the words seemed to come out of my mouth without my permission.

For a moment, he looked as though I'd physically struck him. Then his expression hardened. "Respect, Katie. Have some respect for your father."

All the years. The years of excuses and neglect. The years of holding my tongue and stuffing my emotions shredded my self-control.

"Oh I do, Dad. I respect everything about you. But I particularly respect your addiction—it's been more of a parent to me than you have." I couldn't have held back the words any more than I could have stilled my next heartbeat. Since last night, my feelings had been simmering and now they'd boiled over.

Jewel made noises like a pained hound. "Hymie. Kathryn. Please don't say things that you'll regret."

"I think it's a little late for that, Jewel," my father said, his voice more controlled now. "I'm only trying to tell you that you can't judge a marriage from the outside. Just because they didn't look to be ideally suited for each other didn't mean that they weren't. Just because she doesn't appear to be affected by his death doesn't mean she isn't."

Somehow I realized he wasn't just speaking of the Waites' marriage anymore.

"Dad?"

"Not now, Katie. I'm going to bed early, I think. Thanks for the cake, Jewel." He brushed a kiss across her cheek before he left the room.

Jewel turned to me. Her eyes glistened with tears. My chin rose.

She cleared her throat and said, "I'd best be going." At the doorway, she turned. Instead of scolding me as I had expected, she pulled me into a snug embrace. "Remember, Kathryn," she said hoarsely in my ear, ''you aren't the only one with regrets. I love you, Kathryn.''

And she was gone.

Charli and I left the house shortly after that. I couldn't stay there—not under the same roof with him. I didn't want to think about right or wrong. I didn't want to consider anyone else's side of things. Just once, I wanted to be allowed an honest reaction uncolored by concern for other people's sensibilities or my fear of abandonment.

Dusk proved to be a painted sky of variegated colors: tangerine, aqua, teal, and dove grey. The scalloped clouds rested above the horizon like layers on a birthday cake. The final glimpses of the sun's departure heralded a drop in temperature, which made me long for a jacket of some sort. I decided to swing by the office building where Mary Waite and Victor Stempniak worked.

It was of newer construction located in downtown Landview, one of those buildings that housed everything from orthodontists to beauty salons. A glassed-in directory said that Stempniak Inc., financial advisors and brokers, resided in Suite 2B. There was no security service, so that even at this time of night I was able to traverse the hallways without being detained or appearing conspicuous. When I reached my destination, the telltale glow of indoor lighting suggested that someone might be putting in late hours. Victor? Mary? I recalled that many folks in such careers took advantage of the later time periods to work via a computer with the Far East, making transactions in Japan on the other side of the world.

Fortunately, Charli resisted the urge to snarf the bottom of the doorway and detect who was inside. They might have noticed, and it really wouldn't have helped anyway since the dog remained verbally challenged. He could hardly say, "It's the two of them. I smell men's cologne and soft, feminine gestures."

Standing for a moment to get a sense of what the place felt like, I had an image of late evening conferences. Coffee ordered in. Chinese food. The two of them working congenially together, while Gene no doubt got himself to bed after watching a bit of television with a bowl of popcorn as a companion. Or was he? Could it be that Gene Waite had not been the man I believed him to be? The thought made my eyes lose focus for a moment, as I teetered between loyalty and suspicion.

"Let's go," I told the dog. I'd little desire to be caught in the hallway and another idea had occurred to me that might be helpful. I assumed that Mary, and concurrently Victor, had an alibi for the night Gene was killed, but I wanted to check it out. Perhaps Cole would continue his sudden streak of cooperation.

Meanwhile, on the off chance that Mary Waite might have been behind that office door with or without Victor, I decided to take the opportunity to do a little clandestine snooping. Thus far, I'd not taken advantage of my key to the Waites' home, but for some reason I felt as though time were folding over me like an envelope. If I didn't act quickly, any possibility for acquiring information would be sealed forever.

"What do you think, Charli?" I asked as we drove through downtown Landview. Pockets of teenagers huddled here and there, cruising, waiting to be told to find somewhere else to go—like someone's unsupervised home or the depths of secret alleys, where much more than conversation could take place. Misplaced Chicagoans sipped their cappuccinos outside the coffee house pretending they were in the city and simply missing the lakefront. Outside a bar, a herd of gleaming motorcycles hugged the elbow of the curb, looking as though they were a sales display and not a collection of big-boy toys.

The dog took it all in with the interest of someone who felt grateful to be smelling something other than the neighborhood dogs. I cracked Charli's window more fully so he could stick his entire head out. With the wind blowing his ears like streamers and his eyes weeping against the air rushing by, he appeared the picture of canine joy. If I'd done nothing else tonight, I would have managed to make my dog happy.

Bass honking and sudden wailing told me to pull over to the right. Charli and I stared with equal interest as a fire engine, a Landview ambulance, and a mid-sized car sporting a red flasher swept by. Something akin to civic pride pierced my jaded veneer for a moment. I'm a sucker for parades, too.

"We'll just drive by Gene's house. If it looks vacant, I'll see if I can find that box of Fuzzy Wuzzies." *Or anything else of interest*, I added to myself.

The wind must have taken a turn, because it smelled like the steel mills during an ozone alert. As I entered the Waite neighborhood, the air seemed to hold something else as well—the taut expectation of many souls. I felt as though the temperature had risen ten degrees. It grew noisy. Cars had begun parking in the few available street slots flanking me. As I crept closer, my way was barred entirely by a police officer swinging a flashlight to urge me away from the intersection. People flowed down the sidewalks, comrades created by a shared interest in disaster. Charli barked when they came too close.

The street proved full. I slipped the van in front of someone's driveway and slammed the gear into park.

A house fire tainted the night. The roar of the hoses. The muffled calls of the spectators. The cries of the firefighters.

Sweeping past the crowd, Charli and I raced down the block. I couldn't tell which house was burning. Curds of smoke were now apparent against the indigo night, caught in the reflection of the disinterested streetlamps and the fire department's stark headlights.

I pressed forward, barely grasping Charli's collar before he dodged the front line of spectators and intruded on the fire scene.

A demon blaze engulfed what was left of Mary and Gene's roof.

Chapter Eleven

Flames licked the sky, wicked and selfish. The hissing of the water striking it sounded like a thousand snakes. I searched the front yard, terrified that Mary had been home, injured, or . . . killed.

Standing stoic and strangely beautiful, Mary waited on the sidewalk. A neighbor had draped a brightly colored quilt around her shoulders. An elderly woman seemed to be urging her to come further away from the house. Mary didn't seem to hear. She clutched something to her breast that glinted silver as though it were a shield.

"Mrs. Waite?" I said, reaching her side. "Mary?"

The woman turned to me, her eyes staring at something six inches to the left of my face. I glimpsed simple cotton pajamas beneath the quilt and something else. Shield indeed. Mary Waite was clutching the photograph that I had noticed of her and Gene from their bedroom. She didn't seem to be aware of it.

"It seems," she began, clearing her throat, "that I won't be requiring your services after all, Kathryn."

I didn't know what to say. Her distant monotone could have been shell shock or a fine performance. Whatever clues had been in that house were gone now. Forever.

Suddenly parting the crowd like a knife through butter, Lizzie Waite appeared. She'd taken the time to dress, although her Armani raincoat swept around her like golden water. Perhaps her mother had phoned her. The police or fire personnel might have asked Mary if there was anyone that she needed. However she was summoned, Lizzie had complied.

Frank horror blanched her thin face. I could nearly see the scarlet destruction as flickering reflections in her pupils. She stopped next to her mother, and their resemblance proved uncanny. Charli offered a soft whine as though he were experiencing her loss, the total destruction of her childhood home.

Like a fractured mirror, Lizzie's composure shattered. Burying her face in her hands, she began weeping, agonizing, heart-wrenching sobs. They pierced my heart like daggers. I watched mutely as her mother stood unmoved, clutching her photograph, staring at the flames.

Eventually, a firefighter escorted Lizzie to one of the ambulances, no doubt offering her some support. Mary was speaking to a fire lieutenant while the rest of the crew began cleaning up, hauling in hose, and checking over the remains of the house. I recognized a fellow that I'd done a summer shift with at All Terrain Landscaping. He'd been working on his days off, and I'd been trying to keep myself in art supplies.

"Jimbo," I called carefully. I didn't wish to draw attention to myself or my interest in the firefighter.

"Eh, Kathryn," he answered, sweeping off his helmet and shaking his head as though he were a wet dog. "What y'all doin' chasin' ambulances?"

I nodded at the house. "They were clients. I was selling some merchandise for them."

"Well, babe," he said, offering his cockeyed grin. "Maybe they'll keep you on for the fire sale."

"Maybe." I peered around him to the blackened foundation of the house. "What do you think happened, anyway?"

"No mystery here," he replied, walking toward his comrades. "Broken basement window, gasoline stink. Molotov cocktail for sure."

"A Molotov cocktail?"

"Yeah, it's when ya—"

"I know what it is, Jimbo," I interrupted. "Why would anyone want to . . . ?"

I didn't bother finishing my own question. Why, indeed.

Perhaps it would be worthwhile to offer Lizzie a shoulder to cry on, a place to stay, a listening ear. I stood there struggling to decide if I were more coward than sleuth. I'd no desire to subject myself to that level of emotion and grief. On the other hand, here was a rare opportunity to pick the brain of a possibly vulnerable suspect. Of course, there was always the chance that Lizzie had done the clumsy yet effective bombing and now was covering her tracks with crocodile tears. While I attempted making up my mind, Charli made it up for me. He hastened over to where Lizzie sat on the step to the back of a Landview ambulance and offered her ''snout support.''

''Ugh!'' she exclaimed, pushing him away as though he were the slobbering type, which he is not. ''Go away.''

''Sorry,'' I said, snapping my fingers to call Charli off. ''He was only trying to say he was sorry.''

Lizzie seemed to search the crowd for a moment. Mary wasn't in sight.

A jagged cry brought a fresh onslaught of tears. ''I'm single, my father's dead, my mother might as well be, and a dog is sorry for me,'' she rasped out at last. ''I need a Valium.''

''I'm sorry as well, Lizzie,'' I said gently. ''Is there anything I can do for you? Anyone I can call?''

She gazed up at me. Her eyes looked black and gouged from her destroyed mascara. ''No, Kathryn,'' she said, obviously collecting herself as she stood. ''There's no one.''

I felt hatred and resentment wafting off her like a swamp odor.

She sniffled and tipped her nose skyward. ''Not anymore. Not anymore.''

* * *

Walking slowly back toward my van, her words clung to me like sticky fingers. *No one. No more. No body. No more.* What was the story in that family? Had Lizzie been a beloved daughter? Had Mary been more rival than mother to the girl? Had Gene been the sort of father and husband who bred contempt rather than devotion? Whatever sort of family it had been, it was only the rotting hulk of one now. The carcass of their family had become beached litter for the public domain, their insides fodder for community gossip.

By the time Charli and I reached the van, I felt as though I might have lived several lifetimes in one day. So much had happened. My new house. My new "neighbor," Phil. Gene's memorial. My fight with Dad. The house fire. I was tired. Bone weary. There was little left to do except go home and go to bed.

It would have been unnatural not to stand on the curb of the Sears home and stare at it as though to fix it in my mind indelibly. Etched against the sky, it proved singular in that it was unique from the brick Cape Cods around it. It always had held an aura of isolation, as though our family didn't merit more than wooden siding and that difference was somehow inferior.

A train moaned on its way to somewhere else. Another train seemed to commiserate with it. I glimpsed a telltale light burning in my father's room, and I wondered if, despite his early retirement to his bed, he had stayed up to lose himself in a book.

I rolled the kinks out of my shoulders and went into

the house. The scent of pineapple lingered among the memories as I made my way grudgingly up the stairs. For once, Charli seemed inclined to let me stay in the lead. The landing loomed ahead of me like an unfamiliar harbor following a tortuous journey. It was as though I would not pass this way again.

To the right lay my studio and my art, my future. To the left, lay my father's bedroom and our unfinished business. I turned left.

A soft knock on the door elicited no response.

"Dad?" I called gently, easing the door open a crack.

Charli, as though sensing the import of my visit, remained in the hallway. My father sat in an easy chair beneath the framed photos of his beloved deceased poodle, Paul Mitchell. Wearing his sleeveless T-shirt and boxer shorts, he seemed somehow vulnerable and grey.

"Dad?" I repeated, stepping into the room.

Finally, he appeared to hear me. He glanced up and it was then that I noticed he was holding something— a photograph, an old photograph.

With only the lack of a rebuff as an invitation, I crossed the room and leaned against the windowsill. A streetlamp cast the neighborhood in a maize stage-like glare. The maple beside the partially opened window slid its fingers across the glass.

I didn't know where to begin. Words had never come easily between us, probably due to my fear that scenes such as tonight's would have been the result.

"It's all right, Katie," he said before I could go on.

"You were right. Everything you said was true. I'm a coward. I'm a drunk. And the booze was more of a father to you than I was."

I winced at the word "drunk," more at his tone than the truth of it. Wanting to close the distance between us and kneel beside him, I crossed my arms instead. "That was before. It's not like that any more . . . is it?" I asked tightly.

His eyes shot up to meet mine. Sorrow-diluted pride shone in them. "No," he said. "It isn't."

"Then where did you go when you left the emergency room?"

He didn't reply. Instead, he put aside the picture and gazed out the window behind me. "It was that place. That night. Did I want a drink? Sure. Is there a day that goes by that I don't? No, Katie, there isn't. I wish I could say I was free, but I'll never be."

I could tell he thought his admission would diminish him in my eyes. Instead, I felt grudging admiration for the battle he fought and won every day of his life.

"Tonight," he went on, "when you spoke about Mary Waite, I couldn't help thinking of all the talk there'd been when your mother had died."

This time I did cross the room. I sat cross-legged at his feet, but he didn't seem to notice. His words were as much to himself as to me. "She was lucky, they said, to be free of me at last. I'd have driven her to her grave myself sooner or later. It had only been a matter of time. Eventually, I'd have come home drunk and . . ."

"But you didn't, Dad," I interrupted. The sting of gossip had hounded me, too. Gossip of a different sort.

He stood and shook off my hand, which I'd put on his forearm. "But I could've. That truck driver could've been me. Don't you see? It was only a miracle that I never killed anyone as often as I drove drunk out of my mind. Divine retribution, that's what it was. God took your mother for my sins."

Appearing lost in his private hell, he continued, "I didn't even get to see her one last time. When I should have been by her side, holding her hands . . . feeling her final breath on my cheek . . . I was drunk. Keeping company with a bottle. I lost those moments as I'd lost a thousand others some place where I was nothing, except a joke."

His voice fell to a hush as his forehead furrowed. "I never touched a drop after that, but it didn't matter. She was gone. My angel was gone."

I stood stiffly. While I'd been hiding in my mother's hope chest, struggling to come to terms with her death, he'd been going through his own battles. We'd never discussed how he'd finally gotten sober or why.

"Dad," I said, slipping toward him, "she died because a truck driver was tired, careless, and drunk, not because we were being punished." My glance shifted carelessly to the photograph he'd been holding, their wedding picture. Mother looking so young and bright and hopeful. Dad looking so proud.

"People don't die as a punishment to others," I said, perhaps coming to that conclusion myself for the first time.

He turned to me, his jaw clenching with emotion. "We loved each other, Katie. More than anyone ever knew. They couldn't understand why she stayed. Sometimes I couldn't either. I just knew that I would have died without her. I nearly did."

My eyes squeezed shut. I swallowed hard. "Dad," I said at last, opening my arms.

"Katie."

I wasn't a little girl. In fact, he was a good inch shorter than I. But we held each other and cried openly together for the first time about the loss we'd both endured. The vestiges of my resentment flowed freely with my tears. Dad softened in my arms as though the years of guilt had been a second skin that had been torturously tight and that he was shedding at last.

"Oh, Katie, I love you so. I've tried to be a good father. I've tried to make it up to you."

"Hush, hush. It's all right. I love you, Daddy. It's all right." I held him as tightly as I could. "It's all right."

The following day proved peculiarly bright, rather like blown glass—delicate and refractive. I'd fallen into a dreamless sleep the night before that had left me feeling hollow, empty, and somehow purged. Charli had nestled in the single bed beside me. His warm body and steady breathing was a living comfort in the dawn.

As consciousness seeped back into my body from my slightly chilled toes, through my limbs, and higher, I thought anew of how I would never forget last night.

A part of me wondered if I had the courage to paint it. A portrait of my father. If I could capture him, my perceptions of him, it would be the finest of the series . . . even if I never shared it with anyone and kept the work to myself.

Charli groaned and opened one eye. He shifted onto his back and awaited some stomach stroking. His paws hung in the air like white rabbit's feet. Petulantly, he rolled back after I scissored over him to my desk. I had a mission.

Leafing through a phone book, I shoved my hair behind my ears.

"Time to put this case into high gear, Charli," I decided. "I've fooled around long enough." My overly developed sense of responsibility no doubt held me culpable for the fire last night. After all, had I "solved" the crime sooner, maybe Mary Waite would still have a house. Maybe I would have found those missing Fuzzy Wuzzies and somehow cleared Gene's reputation.

It wasn't difficult to locate the telephone entry plus address that I was looking for. I dressed swiftly. Going for the inconspicuous look, I donned some great khakis, a white shell, and a cast-off designer jacket cinched at the waist. One of the best parts of my work is harvesting my eclectic wardrobe. Because I could hardly leave behind the perfect hat, I donned the Panama number that I'd bought last year. It was inconspicuous, if you consider unicorns down Main Street inconspicuous.

Breakfast could wait. I didn't want to miss him. Charli barely had time for his morning duty before I was in the van and driving off. I would have had a tough time locating the place if I hadn't spent a winter working as a pizza deliverer. That experience had given me a better than average sense for locating Landview addresses. Sometimes I believe the thing that the cops resent the most about me is my cache of information, which I can garner from my many former part-time jobs and associates. That was probably why Cole had asked me to nose around. He must have been really eager for results if he had elicited my help, I considered.

The apartment complex where Brad Paladin lived was only accessible from one main road and several parking lots. Individual units within the rows of boxed-in four-flats were a pain to find as there was no designated parking and half the numbers were worn off the buildings. Nevertheless, I took my best shot at guessing which building was his, and I got lucky.

The rusted Pinto sat beneath a morning sheen of dew, awaiting the call of its owner.

Easing the van into a parking place behind the detached cab of a semi, I moved the seat back a little to wait comfortably.

"Cole probably knows where the guy lives," I told Charli, removing my safety belt. "But he might not have time or manpower to tail him. *I've* got more time than sense, but don't repeat that to anyone."

Morning radio kept us company. Doctor Laura told a single father to buck up and shut up. Deepak Chopra suggested we listen to our inner voice. And a Dominick's advertisement hawked eggs for forty-five cents a dozen through Friday. My stomach growled noisily. Or maybe that was Charli's.

"Look," I said, straightening. A redheaded man, sans the goatee, emerged from the building to the left of the one that I had targeted. Even without his facial hair I recognized Brad. He appeared tidier than he had on the fleeting occasions that I'd seen him before. Nevertheless, he seemed preoccupied as he unlocked his car door and got in the Pinto.

Tailing suspects is not my forte. It's tough to blend in when you drive a company van, but I intended to try. A wide belt of abandoned land encircled the apartments. I had to let Brad reach the stop sign, which heralded a neighborhood of single-family dwellings, before I even started my vehicle. Then, mentally crossing my fingers for luck, I took off after him.

Fortunately, he wasn't a particularly observant person or he would have pegged me half a dozen times. Since his location proved to be within five miles of his apartment, I didn't have time to screw up more often than that.

I sat on the street as the Pinto disappeared around a corner of the employees' parking lot of the Lucky Star dish factory, Corelle's first real competitor in the daily-use dish market. Charli nudged me under the arm as if to say, "Are you satisfied? Can we have breakfast now?"

Putting the car into gear, I grinned. Cole probably knew where Paladin worked and found the fact unremarkable.

"Let's go get something to eat," I told the dog.

Making a U-turn, I headed back to Halstead and enough restaurant choices to fill a football stadium. "I need to give our next move a little more thought, and I don't sleuth well on an empty stomach."

The Pancake House offered moderate resistance to seating Charli and me. My assurance that I was visually impaired, if not legally blind, and a five-dollar bill procured us a booth by the back door. In an attempt to recoup my five-dollar investment, I ordered the bargain harvest special: two pancakes, two waffles, two eggs, two slices of toast, hash browns, and juice. I drank the juice and picked at the pancakes. Charli gobbled the rest.

By the time he had licked every bit of strawberry syrup off his plate, which I had discretely slipped under the table, and begun cleaning his paws like a cat, I had my plans formulated. Less than a mile away, I stopped at a florist to procure my props. The actress in me was in the green room. I was psyched for my part.

Driving to the front entrance of the Lucky Star business office at the front of the factory, I left Charli in the van. Carrying my purchase, a pathetic philodendron in a chintzy pot topped by a dopey miniature Mylar balloon, I sauntered into the building.

I took note of the older man, who appeared to be working as the receptionist. I see many senior citizens working in stores all the time. I don't know why I should have been surprised to find a senior citizen at an entry-level position in a dish factory, but I was.

"May I help you, young lady?" he asked, looking

dapper with his gold-tipped-string lariat tie and matching collar tips on his neatly pressed white short-sleeved shirt. He folded his chunky hands in front of a couple of multipurpose phones. On his ring finger a hefty diamond winked at me.

"Yes, sir," I said sprightly. "I have a delivery here for one of your employees."

"Isn't that special?" the man said, sitting tall. There didn't seem to be an ounce of fat on him, and I felt increasingly curious why such a robust, impoverished man would be taking other people's phone calls. Nevertheless, I proceeded with my script.

"Do you have a name?" he asked.

I made a show of checking the sheet on my fake ordering pad. "Brad Paladin," I answered.

"Paladin. Paladin. I don't seem to recall that name. Hold on just a minute." Pivoting in his seat as though he'd just turned his mare, the man adroitly typed some information into his personal computer, switching screens as easily as flipping pages. "Here he is. Brad Paladin. He hasn't been with us that long. That's why I didn't recognize the name. Working in receiving and delivering."

I made a mental note of that.

"You can leave it here with me," the man said, standing. "I'll see that he gets it."

I pulled the pot back a bit toward me. "I'm sorry." Sweetest smile. "But I have to deliver it personally. It's accompanied by a singing message."

A twinkle alighted in his eye. "And *you* would be doing the singing?"

"Yes," I answered breathlessly. Before he could ask me any further questions that I hadn't rehearsed answers to, I went into the most humiliating part of this shtick: singing.

Had I not been told previously in my life that I carried a tune with all the grace of a rhinoceros doing a waltz, I might have been hurt when he winced and backpedaled toward an office door.

"Just hold on, young lady," the man was able to interject before my big refrain. "I'll need to get authorization."

I offered him a dazzling smile and as soon as he was out of the room hightailed it back to the van. The performer in me couldn't help feeling proud of my little show and disappointment that I'd been denied my finale.

As we sped away, I told Charli, "I suppose I should give Cole a call now."

The dog didn't answer.

A red light left us sucking the exhaust fumes of a tanker truck. I felt tremendous satisfaction at discovering that Brad Paladin was employed by Dick Chase. And he worked in receiving and delivering, too. Yep. Lucky Star was Dick Chase's primary business when he wasn't dedicating parks . . . or chasing Fuzzy Wuzzies. Whodahthunk?

A sharp rap on the passenger's window startled me. Of course, my guard dog offered nary a whimper as the man from Lucky Dish reception said seriously, "Young lady, I think you forgot something."

He opened the door and eased his bulk in. He nodded ahead, indicating the light had turned green. I assumed that he intended that I should drive on—with him. "Didn't you?" he finished.

Chapter Twelve

It seemed that I had company. Either the red light had taken longer than I'd realized or my hijacker was some sort of marathon runner who didn't perspire. A car parked hastily at the road side suggested that he'd merely hopped into his Buick and caught up with me. Why?

"Where are we going?" I asked, dropping the innocent act. Charli had made way for the guy without so much as a whimper of protest. Maybe I should investigate security training for that dog?

"Just keep driving down this road," he told me, nodding south.

This was not going according to my plan. I hate it when things don't go according to my plans. He didn't look particularly dangerous, but I've been wrong before. I tried considering my options as I drew abreast of a police cruiser at the stoplight. As surreptitiously as I could, I nodded and winked at the officer to indicate that my companion was not welcome. The young cop merely looked flattered, tipped an imaginary hat, and drove on. The guy next to me chuckled.

"Turn here," he said, pointing.

"Again." He gestured at a rolling cemetery thick with trees that abutted the limestone quarry. I thought of being tossed to my death, tumbling into that vast stone chasm, and began to worry legitimately. Besides, I like cemeteries less than I like emergency rooms, although admittedly this one held a certain artistic appeal with its curious headstones and occasionally ornate mausoleum.

He indicated that I should stop the van at the top of a mound where a black wrought-iron fence defined a family plot as though it were a secret garden. English ivy crept wantonly over a concrete bench inside, and some sort of speckled vine spilled over the tops of matching runs.

I purposely didn't turn off the engine. He reached over and did so for me, tossing the keys in the air, and landing them in his beefy palm before his fingers closed tight around them.

"So, young lady," he began. "Let's have a little talk."

I said nothing.

He gave me a good look over. Charli gave him a good look over. I willed the dog to do something menacing, but he seemed fascinated by those gold wing tips. Charli is a sucker for fine jewelry.

"What would a pretty gal like you be doing pretending to deliver flowers?" he asked, turning slightly toward me.

"I was delivering flowers. I sing and I deliver flowers and, well, I had to use the lady's room . . ."

"I don't think so. You left with the flowers."

"I would have been back. As a matter of fact, I still need a lavatory. Why don't we just head back out of here and find one?"

"Why don't you pull the blinders off and quit thinking that'm buying any of your whoppers? I didn't live to be seventy-eight by letting little girls tap dance on my logic."

He didn't look seventy-eight . . . and I was no "little girl."

This was getting us nowhere. I no longer felt any real threat to my person, yet I suspected that I wasn't getting my keys back until I'd satisfied this guy's curiosity. Only one defense left. A good offense.

"Who are you? You don't seem to be an average receptionist. Aren't you going to get in trouble leaving the phones unattended?" A pair of blackbirds burst from a nearby evergreen and scaled upward.

He seemed to consider my request. "I'll make you a deal. I'll tell you what you want to know over dinner."

"Dinner?"

The guy grinned. He was the best looking seventy-eight-year-old I had ever seen. "Darn little entertains me at this point in my life, but I believe you do. Why don't you let me buy you a thick tenderloin and you can tell me why you're creeping around my son-in-law's company?''

''Your son-in-law?'' My jaw might have dropped two inches before I called it back into position.

''Yes,'' he answered with what might have been a trace of annoyance. ''Dick Chase.''

He thrust his hand toward me. ''How do you do? I'm Hugh Rogers. Just in for a little visit and you seem more interesting than Judge Judy and Court TV.''

Call me stupid, but I shook his hand and answered truthfully, ''Melody Joy. . . .'' All right, I decided not to be entirely truthful. ''. . . This lady gave me twenty dollars to deliver the flowers and find out where the Paladin guy worked.''

Hugh Rogers ceased to look entirely social, instead a somewhat weary expression mixed with concern altered his countenance. ''Horned toads and chili peppers. I wonder what's going on now? So you work for this Good Buys?''

It's so difficult being clandestine in the company van. Perhaps my hesitation fueled his suspicion.

''Look, honey. I'm not going to hurt you. Dick just tends to get himself into messes and I worry about little Becky that's all. My granddaughter. If there's something going on at Lucky Star, I'd be obliged if you told me.''

Oh, decisions, decisions. I scanned the silent stones witnessing this peculiar meeting. ''Why don't I explain over that dinner you offered?'' I answered. We made arrangements to meet that evening at Gino's

Steak House and thankfully he let me drive me back to his Buick without incident.

"See you later," he said, tipping his head at me through the window.

"Bye," I replied, a frozen, a freon smile on my face.

As I drove away, I could see him studying my retreat. Minimum, I'd bought myself some time to check *him* out. He might be slightly protective or admittedly bored, but he was now a wild card in my deck. Fifty-two card pick-up, anyone?

I love the Internet. Although I had been admittedly reluctant to enter the world of personal computers, an introduction to playing in "font land" had gotten me over the hump of my resistance. As time passed, I had learned to appreciate the delights of the database, and while I prefer using my snitches, there's nothing like a search engine for locating the occasional Texan. For some reason, I suspected my dinner date of hailing from the Lone Star State.

Picking at a piece of leftover pineapple upside down cake, I sat in my bedroom and moved into "techno detecting." My old PC was as plodding as a Clydesdale and nearly as dependable. There was something endearing to me about the way it grunted between tasks.

Bingo. Hugh Rogers was best known for an aborted race for governor in the early eighties. Apparently, some sort of family crisis had caused him to drop out of the primaries. Dick Chase must have married into the Lucky Star business, because that and a now-defunct chain of fried-chicken restaurants had earned Hugh Rogers his fortune. The only recent thing of information that I could glean from the Net was that Hugh Rogers had sunk a good deal of resources more recently into extraterrestrial research. Funny, he didn't seem the type.

"Well, Charli," I said, pressing my fork into the crumbs on my plate to snatch every last bit of cake, "what do you suppose we should do next?"

He raised his ears and looked at me speculatively. Canting his head to the side, he offered the impression that he was waiting for me continue.

I obliged him. "We have until seven o'clock before we can pump our dinner date for information on just what kind of scrapes his son-in-law has gotten himself into. Sifting through the ashes of Gene's home would probably not be fruitful, and frankly I have no interest in searching out Lizzie."

I stood and stretched, luxuriating in the little pops my spine made when I twisted from side to side. The Fuzzy Wuzzy Britt I'd bought caught my eye. I picked it up from the nest of old correspondence upon which it lay. Cute little thing. As I "worked" the toy the way I'd been instructed to, I felt more tension relax. My mind floated freely. I took the little critter with me into my studio and plopped into the recliner. Rolling and rolling. Musing and relaxing. Some old song, about Fuzzy Wuzzy no longer having hair, trickled through my mind like a shallow stream over worn stone.

The stream began growing clearer. It developed a

beginning. In my mind's eye, I viewed a case of Fuzzies. Further down the stream, I saw Dick and Becky Chase. They ran from the stream to the line at Preston's to the park outside of town. In their arms, a bundle of Fuzzies threatened to spill over into the water. Thirty feet from them I glimpsed Brad Paladin. He watched the Chases and the Fuzzies. Even further downstream, I perceived Gene. He sat on the edge of the water and fished. Instead of catching fish, he kept pulling in Fuzzies.

Charli and I sneaked past Gene to where the water seemed to pick up speed. Finally, we arrived at a waterfall. Staring over the tumbled rush of water into the surprisingly churning pool below, I saw an entire slew of helpless Fuzzies whirling and eddying as though they might drown. On all sides, the flea marketers and Gladys, Mary, Victor, and Lizzie all dipped and snatched at the water, trying to snag one. They failed miserably.

My consciousness drifted back to the world of my room.

Obviously, Becky and Dick were collectors or they wouldn't have tried bribing people at the Preston's line. Maybe I could somehow reach Becky and get further info out of her, I considered, as I slung my leg over the arm of the chair. Across the room, the beginnings of "Gertrude" pinioned me. Guilt began chipping at my determination to solve the case. I'd an invitation to a New York gallery and I was not painting—not at all.

If Paladin had swiped the missing case of Fuzzies

from beneath Chase's nose, had Gene offered to help him? I could imagine a scenario where Gene held the box for Paladin without knowing the contents, but I still couldn't believe that he had knowingly accepted stolen goods.

I got up and paced the room. My paints called me. Conflicting urges charged my imagination. When I found myself preparing my oils, there remained a flight of a fancy that winged its way beyond the walls of my studio. Somehow, Gene had met someone, someone he knew, late at night. That person or someone else had killed him. Where were the Fuzzies now? Closing my eyes against the ebony void of my perplexity, I gathered my artist self.

With one stroke, I had shoved the investigation to the side. With two strokes, I had lost touch with my surroundings. By the third stroke, my own house could have gone up in flames and I probably wouldn't have noticed.

Ah, Gertrude. I studied the partially rendered painting in front of me. Gertrude Trent, former client and forever a friend, studied me back. Mystically, I'd captured the keen intelligence in her eyes and the compelling strength in her face. I wished I could call Gertrude for input on this case, but her last postcard suggested that she was traveling in Turkey with an old friend. Ideally, she wouldn't take a side trip and try to straighten out Saddam Hussein while she was in the Middle East.

I searched my work in progress clinically. Satisfaction streamed through my veins like a sweet elixir. Nothing. Nothing felt more gratifying than a vision rendered faithfully. For a moment, I lost myself in the thick ox-blood red, variegated jade, and shimmering oyster colors on the canvas. While the work was clearly a portrait, the background of the painting raged around it, vibrant and compelling. The painting, an amalgamation of sundry styles, resulted in something totally original. While different in content than my previous series, the work held the same wild attentive detail and nature-born impressions. It was a Kathryn Bogert, I realized with satisfaction.

"Katie?" I heard my father call from downstairs. "I'm home."

"Down in a little while, Dad," I hollered back. Charli tripped off to greet "the old man."

As I had no clock in my studio, I could only assume that I'd worked for hours. My dinner with Hugh wasn't until seven and since tonight was goulash night and I was starving and my father would be wanting to place a culinary seal on our latest reconciliation, I decided to eat twice.

Following a revitalizing shower, I dressed for my rendezvous with Hugh. The Steak House called for an upscale look. I donned a blue pin-striped pants suit, black silk camisole, peacock-fabric boutonniere, and some honest to goodness spats. One of the best things about my work is filling my plate with a sumptuous variety of estate leftovers.

Dad offered a wolf whistle when I entered the kitchen. "*Now* what?"

"Don't 'birth bovine' on me," I replied. "My date isn't until later. Right now, goulash sounds fabulous."

" 'Birth bovinely?' "

"Have a cow," I translated.

My father began building a heaping plateful of his specialty for me. "It'd be a crime to waste a fine meal like this," he said, waxing Jewish. "If I should die, make sure that you never lose Aunt Enna's goulash recipe."

"I promise, Dad."

During our repast, I filled my father in on my activities of that day. Afterwards, he asked to see my painting.

"Oh, Katie," he said, his arm around my shoulders as we stood just inside the door of my studio, "you've got a gift. A real gift. It's wonderful, sweetheart. Really wonderful."

"Thanks, Dad." I could see a million places now that required correction.

"Have you contacted that gallery yet?" Dad continued, nonchalantly pulling at his left ear. "If you want, I could give them a ring for you. Set a few things up."

"No, I have not given them a call and you do not have to set things up," I replied, tweaking his cheek.

He looked so disappointed that I added, "I'll call them soon, all right?"

"New York, Katie," he said, beaming. "Big time. Your mother always wanted to see a real Broadway musical," he added to my surprise. Until last night we had never discussed the past.

"Really?" I asked, looping my arm through his as we made our way back downstairs.

"Absolutely. She was a music lover, your mother. And her voice. Like a songbird she could sing."

He kept talking, sharing one story after another. I sat across from him in the living room and listened while my mother's voice singing "The Lullaby of Broadway" played counterpoint in my head. Memories, like holiday aromas, filled the room, drenching me in sweet remembrance. Once again, I blessedly forgot about Gene Waite and the Fuzzy Wuzzies.

"Melody Joy," Dick said, sawing at his tenderloin. "A fellow could forget his Mama's maiden name talking to you. You are not only the prettiest thing it's been my privilege to dine with, but the most amusing."

I rearranged the food on my plate. Portions at Gino's East did not allow for goulash appetizers. Dad's repast had dulled my appetite considerably.

This evening, my host wore a spruced-up version of his earlier getup. This time, he'd added a suit jacket and cowboy hat. True to his millinery heritage, he kept the hat with him, although not on his head during dinner, like a true Texan.

"And it is my pleasure to tell you . . ."—he paused to partake of a swallow of wine—"that I don't believe your reputation does you justice."

"Reputation?"

"Yes, Miss Bogert. You are not a bad sneak." He winked at me. "But I'm better, agreed?"

I speared my asparagus, but not to eat it. Sighing, I leveled him a gaze. "You've had more experience."

"True."

"So," Dick said, shoving his empty platter to the side, "what has my son-in-law got himself into now? What's he done to attract the interest of Landview's finest amateur detective?"

Chapter Thirteen

My cocky gaze slipped several notches into barely secure. "Detective?"

"Miss Bogert," he continued, his hands on the table. I noticed that despite the huge diamond ring, his hands retained a solid workman's appearance. Hard-earned calluses and the scarred nicks of a laborer's life adorned fists that would have done a prize fighter proud. I entertained a gruesome image of myself as a punching bag beneath his not-infirm questions.

I evaluated my options. I could leave. What would he charge me with? Impersonating a flower deliverer? Freeloading a steak? What if his country-gentleman act was no more legitimate than my little performance? This good ol' boy might be in the thick of whatever nefarious activities Dick Chase was involved in.

Beginning to swing my legs to the side so as to exit the booth, his deep voice cut me off. "I wouldn't do that if I were you. What would you say if I told you that I had a magnum pointed right at your fancy fly from under this table?"

I froze. "I'd say that I thought you had been carrying a banana all this time," I said, and gulped.

He didn't laugh.

His eyes turned to steel and a stern expression slipped firmly in place. I eased myself back into the position of a willing and jovial dinner companion.

"That's better," he said. "At my age, you never know when the trigger finger is going to have some kind of pesky tremor."

The bus person appeared to refill our water glasses ostentatiously. Before I could take advantage of the interruption, the girl had whisked off to the next table.

"I apologize for the heavy-handed methods, but I have to be in Dallas by noon tomorrow and I don't have time to pussy foot around." He took a drink of wine with his left hand. I could only assume that the right hand was preoccupied.

"Fuzzy Wuzzies," I said, making a quick decision. I don't like being target practice, and I didn't like his remark about tremors.

Instead of eliciting curiosity or anger, Hugh's face took on an expression of extreme annoyance. "Those darn stupid toys," he said. "He's not trying to sell Becky's collection again, is he?"

Sell *her* collection? Now that was an intriguing possibility. I played along. "Well, it is impressive," I said.

He snorted. "And, it *is* hers. I may not like them, but according to current market value, that child has enough to put herself through college if she needs to, and I mean to make sure that she keeps that option. Especially the way her father goes through money."

"I take it that her father has attempted this before?" Hugh's hands had returned to the table. His empty hands. I looked at them pointedly.

Hugh shrugged his shoulders. "I was bluffing. You're not much of a poker player, are you?"

He was right about that. I never call someone's bluff who might blow me away.

"My daughter was a sweet thing, but she wouldn't recognize a rattlesnake if it were doing the cha-cha at her feet. When she died, I would've taken Becky, except she wanted so bad to be with her Daddy, for that man to love her. One stubborn girl, my Becky."

I imagined the child in my mind's eye and couldn't disagree.

Taking the plunge I asked, "Do you know anything about the fourth edition?"

A mirthless smile appeared. His grey eyes darkened like storm-laden clouds. "So that's what this is about? The fourth edition."

I barely noticed the end of the meal or dessert while Hugh explained to me about what he knew of the missing collection. By the time he was done, I had a pretty clear idea how Gene had been killed. There were still some things I wanted to check, but if the situation was as I suspected, I knew who did the deed. Proving it? That would be another challenge altogether.

The next day, I met with a young woman who had driven up from Muncie to settle her parents' estate. The couple had died tragically in a skiing accident in Utah on their fiftieth wedding anniversary. After sorting through her parents' things for mementos and particulars, she was ready to hire me to liquidate the rest. I felt glad to have the work. After all, even with my savings and a hefty down payment, I was still going to have a mortgage to pay. With luck, I would have the Waite business done by next week and I could devote my full attention to the new account.

By the time we'd finished our business meeting, it was midmorning. I decided to stop by the barbershop and see what Dad was up to. Maybe we could toss around some theories. I parked in the lot around the back and Charli and I made for the entrance.

The dog traipsed happily into the shop to stake his claim on the sun-splashed linoleum beneath the picture window. Dad was completing a sale with an obviously just-shorn customer.

''Thanks, Hymie,'' the fellow said. ''I feel kinda funny buying this here mousse. But my wife says it'll be just the thing for my flyaway hair.''

''Your wife is right again, Bruno. And if you don't like it, you can always use it when you run out of shaving cream.'' Dad laughed at himself. It was a solo act. The customer appeared nebulous.

"Hi, Dad," I said, closing the door behind me.

"Katie!" His face lit up as though a flashlight had blinked on behind it. "Bruno, you've met my daughter, Kathryn. She's a famous artist, you know. If you ever need a topnotch salesperson, she's the one for you."

Bruno mumbled, "Nice to meet you."

I held up pretty well under Dad's effusions, with more patience than usual. Bruno made a hasty exit and I was left alone with my father. His was a two-chair shop, which he'd purchased years before with the intention of hiring another barber. In those days, business had been steady and simple. Currently, Dad had a cadre of loyal customers, who accepted his jurisdictional prerogatives as they would a benevolent ruler's. My father came and went as he pleased and remained the least expensive fine haircut in town.

"Have a seat," Dad said, gesturing to the right of the two empty barber chairs. "Would you like a soda?" I declined and he got himself one from the sturdy machine in the corner. It was an older model. Dad opened it himself and removed an Orange Crush. When I was growing up, I'd felt that there was something delicious about the way he could do that. The machine still intrigued me more than the monoliths of plastic that talked and blinked red-lit information before belching forth any number of the far-flung species of the greater category of "Coke."

"No thanks," I said, plopping myself into the barber chair and crossing one leg over the other. "Here's the latest." I prepared to tell him about Hugh's revelations. Before I could begin, Detective Cole intruded. He sported some kind of Wedgwood button-down shirt that made him look mighty appealing.

"Thought I might find you here," the detective said, acknowledging Charli with a pat on the dog's head.

"Intuition working well?" I quipped.

"Patrol person saw the van," he answered. He gave me one of those long stares that always inclined me to raise my hands in the air and yell, "I didn't do it! Whatever it was." As though he had all the time in the world, he strolled to Dad's bulletin board and studied the local notices with casual interest.

Not for the first time, I wondered why Cole had "invited" me to help the police. Had he actually decided that I was an asset? His next statement clarified the situation mightily.

"You can lay off trying to nose around the Waite situation," he said, sitting on one of the beaten-leather customer's chairs.

I glanced at him with suspicion.

"I've been able to confirm your alibi for the night that he was killed."

"My alibi?" I sputtered.

He leaned forward and loosely folded his hands together between his legs. "Your alibi. Lizzie Waite had tried to implicate you in her father's supposed murder along with her mother."

"But I never gave you an alibi. . . ." My dad was suddenly motionless and quiet. His fingers had tightened around the arms of his chair.

"Just needed a little touch-up, eh detective?" Dad said. "A little small talk before hitting the road."

Dad's flushed complexion told me what I needed to know. While the detective had never asked me where I was the night of Gene's death, he'd apparently gotten the information out of Dad. It must have taken him a while to get a third party to confirm that my father and I had been at an auction in Lake Station.

Cole seemed unconcerned with Dad's feelings.

"You honestly thought that I was guilty of a hit-and-run?" I cried, spinning a bit in the chair.

"I honestly thought that if you knew about Ms. Waite's accusations, you'd be more likely to screw up my investigation than if I sent you off sniffing on my behalf."

Charli stretched on the floor. His stomach growled noisily. Sniffing was, after all, his specialty.

"Besides," Cole went on, "there are some in the department who would be more than happy to see you implicated in a murder."

I thought of Sgt. Randy Burns, but I didn't mention any names.

My eyes narrowed. "Use me and toss me away, will you?"

"Kathryn," Cole said, his voice lowered. "Is that an invitation? Begging your pardon, Mr. Bogert."

My father had apparently decided he liked the double entendre in the detective's repartee. When visions of grandchildren dance in his head, he becomes quite generous.

"No offense taken, T. J.," Dad answered, standing

and leaning against the wall nursing his Orange Crush and watching us as though we were this week's episode of "Baywatch."

"Look, Kathryn," Cole continued, arranging his hands in the shape of a steeple. "I know you. I figured this way I could keep an eye on you and you never know . . . you might stumble on something useful without blowing yourself to bits."

In defense of my snooping skills, I told Cole all about my meeting with Hugh Rogers. Cole told me that he now had a witness to the robbery at the White Hen. The description matched Brad Paladin, but the witness couldn't identify Brad definitively.

"So," my father said, waxing mysterious as he paced the squares on the floor, "we have Brad Paladin robbing a White Hen and stowing the gun in Gene's basement."

"Possibly," Cole conceded.

"And," Dad went on, running his hand over his hair, "we know that Brad worked for Dick Chase when a fourth-edition collection turned up missing. And we've got Dick Chase, who seems a little dirty and mighty interested in Fuzzy Wuzzies."

I let the two men conjugate a few more verbs before setting the entire thing into perspective. "The house burning could have been an attempt by Paladin to destroy any evidence of his activities," I offered. "Sloppy way to clean up loose ends, particularly since we'd already found the gun. Although the way he showed up at the funeral wasn't exactly intelligent either.

"How about this?" I continued rhetorically, standing and walking to the wall mirror. I made a production of securing my barrette. "Hugh Rogers had made arrangements to buy that collection of fourth-edition Fuzzies for Becky, and his son-in-law was one of the few people who knew about it."

"Katie!" Dad cried, snapping his fingers. "Do you think Dick Chase stole the collection from his father-in-law out of the hands of his own child?"

"Apparently, he's tried to use her collection as a bank loan before," I told them both.

Cole had begun staring at me strangely.

"What?" I asked.

A hint of a smile teased his mouth.

"What?" I repeated.

"You didn't blow yourself up," he noted. I hadn't told either of them about Rogers' "kidnapping." It hadn't seemed necessary information. "And you seem to have stumbled onto a bit of useful information."

"High praise."

"Indeed," he answered.

"So," my father went on, barely aware of Cole and me as he talked to himself and alternately took long pulls on his soda, "Paladin could have intercepted the Fuzzies."

"How?" I asked.

"Perhaps it was an accident. The box fell in shipping. Spilled open. Since he knew Gene, he might have known that they were worth something. . . ."

"Although I doubt if he knew their real value," Cole added.

"Gene might have told him later," I said, blanching. I could imagine Gene congratulating Brad on his windfall and hardly suspecting that his former student had come by the goods illegally. "Mary had said that she'd seen a case of Fuzzies in the basement. I didn't find any the next day. How does this sound? Gene is holding the goods for Brad. Brad phones and tells him some kind of story to get him to meet him that night."

"Paladin retrieves the Fuzzy Wuzzies," my father interrupted diabolically, licking his lips, "and Brad runs him over so that no one will ever know the truth."

"Why give them to Gene in the first place?" I asked, fiddling with a flat handle brush. "Why not just sell them right away?"

"For safekeeping. He needed someone to help him price the merchandise and hook him up with a buyer," Cole suggested, slipping a toothpick into his mouth and rolling it from side to side.

"But why Gene?" I reiterated. Then I answered my own question. "Because Gene wouldn't have suspected anything illegal. He would have trusted Paladin." My lip curled. "And that trust got him killed."

"Maybe," Cole said, "and maybe not."

"What do you mean?" I asked. A customer tried to enter the shop. Dad shooed the teenager away and flipped his OPEN sign to read CLOSED.

"This is a lot of supposing," Cole answered, rolling his shoulders as though easing out some tension. "Lots of theories and no proof," he said, tossing his toothpick into a waste receptacle on his way to the door. "None of it would constitute even a warrant, let alone a conviction. Paladin probably did the robbery, but murder? We might never be able to prove what happened to Gene Waite.''

''Giving up?'' I said, taking a step toward him, my hands on my hips.

''Hardly,'' Cole answered, squinting against the noon sun, which was slanting through the glass on the door. ''Simply acknowledging that sometimes the bad guy gets away.''

Cole left.

Not this time, I thought. *Not if I can help it. The police needed proof? I'd get it for them in spades . . . or die trying. Metaphorically speaking, of course.*

It was while eating an individual pizza that I noodled out what I was going to do next. Charli had stared at each cheesy bite as though I were depriving him of his last meal. ''Don't think that because you had pancakes yesterday that I'm going to completely disregard the vet's diet. After all, you wouldn't want the November pin-up Charli to be ten pounds heavier than Dad's January calendar boy.''

Reference to the calendar project made Charli passive. He quit nose-nudging and tried to be as unobtrusive as possible at my feet.

I finished lunch hastily before speaking to the manager. He had remained friendly with me since my delivery days and, while he was a little reluctant, eventually agreed to comply with my request. I had to promise to have dinner with him. Which I would. I simply didn't say when.

Back at home, I donned the delivery shirt and cap that the manager had lent me. A pair of khaki pants completed my transformation into Kathryn, pizza deliverer. A pang of disloyalty accompanied my thought that I should be wearing a Panozzo Pizza uniform. Then I thought of Tommy and dismissed such guilt happily. I was considering whether to leave Charli at home when the doorbell rang. Hastening down the stairs, I flung open the door and discovered Gary standing on the porch, looking debonair in a dress shirt and pants.

"New job?" he asked, taking my appearance in stride. "I've never liked those little hats, but on you it looks good."

We hadn't seen each other since the night of the kiss and the strawberry debacle. I found myself warming to his compliment. "What are you doing here, Gary?" I replied, not unkindly.

He leaned against the door frame and crossed his arms, as I'd not invited him in. "I have a client nearby and some extra time, so I thought I'd swing by and see if I could catch you in."

"That's nice," I said, searching the floor for my backpack. "But I'm actually just on my way out."

"I'll go with you."

"I don't think so."

"You aren't delivering pizza, are you?" he asked, his voice playfully reproachful.

As I formulated a response, he reached forward and pulled my wrists toward him. I'd been attempting to cross my fingers behind my back in preparation for my white lie. He laughed endearingly, obligingly, and gave me a slight tug toward him. My hands rose to his chest and his breath swept my forehead. "I've missed you, Kathryn," he said. His lips replaced his breath on my brow. Contentment heated my flesh and I began feeling soft in his arms.

"Gary," I protested feebly. Even as I allowed him to draw me closer, I continued, "I don't think this is a good . . ."

His mouth settled over mine, innocent at first, then plucking determinedly. Some final shred of resistance eased in my brain and I pressed myself into the kiss. Home. Security. The delicious drumming of my pulse at my neck. He kissed me as though he meant it, and heaven help me, I kissed him back.

Finally, I drew away and settled my cheek beneath his chin. I sighed. "I'm not sure this is such a good idea."

"I am." His arms firmed around me.

"Last time . . ." I began.

"I let you get away," he finished, his hand capturing the nape of my neck and steering my face back toward his. His eyes were determined and vital. "I don't intend to make the same mistake twice."

This time I initiated the kiss, and it felt better than the first time. I discovered his name echoing through my spinning consciousness. His body felt warm and inviting against my own. It was a kiss to build dreams on, and I've such a lively imagination.

"Mmmm," I said at last, abdicating his lips.

He didn't say anything, yet I sensed his self-restraint

in the tautness of his arms. "Have dinner with me," he murmured, his fingertip outlining my kiss-swollen lower lip.

"All right," I answered.

"Tonight," he said firmly.

His change in tone shook me from my reverie. "I can't. Not tonight. I have plans."

"Delivering pizza," he said, fingering the collar of my shirt. Before I could wheedle out an explanation, Gary continued, "I don't think so."

"I *am* delivering pizza." *And snooping around,* I added mentally.

"No doubt." His indulgent look didn't offend me. Instead, I found it endearing. "Why don't you let me go with you? I can call it quits for the day."

Had he tried to strongarm me, he would have gotten nowhere. As it was, when he added, "Come on, it'll be fun," I found myself agreeing. It would be fun . . . and a little dangerous. My favorite sort of fun.

Chapter Fourteen

I liked Gary's apple-red Le Baron convertible. The guy had always had a thing for cars with an attitude. As we drove over to Paladin's apartment complex, I cradled the double-deluxe pizza box in my lap and wondered how Gary was feeling about ''Mr. Mayhem,'' as Phil called Charli, shedding on his backseat upholstery. He didn't seem to notice, instead carrying on a light conversation about where in Chicago I'd like to dine that evening.

My mind was elsewhere. I figured that I had until at least three o'clock before Brad got off his shift at Lucky Star. If there was anyone living with him, I intended to find out. If the place was empty, well, I'd learned a couple of things about breaking and entering. Partnering with a civilian like Gary had certain advantages, after all. There would be no disagreements about ethics, I hoped.

"Now, let me get this straight," Gary said, after backing into a parking place away from a mature maple that really posed no threat of dripping sap. "You're going to gain entrance to the apartment by delivering this pizza."

"Yep," I answered cheerfully. "That and my urgent need to phone headquarters."

"What if . . ." he tried again to inject reason into my plan. Spoilsport.

A swift kiss quieted him. "I'll be fine. You and Charli keep each other company. I'll be back before you know it."

Escaping before Gary could offer further protest, I strode across the parking lot to the entry of the building. My plan was to ring all the doorbells until someone buzzed me in; however, that proved unnecessary. On the first ring, a soft voice answered over the intercom to Brad's apartment.

"Yes?" she said.

"Pizza delivery," I replied, snapping some gum.

"I didn't order pizza," she replied.

I went through a swift check of the address and assured her that a pizza had been bought and paid for by credit card to this address.

"Is it triple cheese and mushroom?" the voice on the other end asked innocently.

"Yep."

"Brad must have ordered it for me," she said, more happy than wary now. "Come on up."

The security buzzer sounded and I turned the doorknob separating the foyer from the rest of the building. I proceeded swiftly to the second floor. At Apartment 2B, I felt myself being eyeballed through the peephole. I tried looking appropriately harried.

The door swung open, revealing a slender, red-haired woman with innocent eyes and a multitude of freckles. She reached eagerly for the pizza and I said, "Where would you like me to put it down?"

"Here, okay?" She gestured at a dining-room table cluttered with paper squares and origami figures of all sizes and shapes and colors. It was then that I noticed mobiles of origami figures flashing from the ceiling. The dining/living room area seemed awash with the paper art. Beneath it all, not so well-made secondhand furniture defined the space. The room wore the tired walls left by a disinterested landlord and carpet remnants that had endured multiple tenants. A smell of mold permeated the air.

"These are nice," I said, picking up an origami frog.

"It jumps. See?" she said eagerly. She pressed the back of the figure and it hopped an inch. "They're special. My brother says I have 'this ability' and that's why the government sends us money every month."

This ability, huh? Disability?

"Brad works very hard to take care of us," she went on. Her lower lip extended childishly and she said, "Brad says that I'm not supposed to let strangers in while he's at work. Brad works very hard. He's going to be famous someday, just like Earnest Hemtheday. He wrote books, you know.''

''I know,'' I replied, guessing this lady's physical age to be early twenties and her emotional age to be much less. ''Brad sounds like a good brother.''

''Oh, Brad's the best,'' she said, beaming. ''He takes me to the movies and buys me popcorn. He just bought us this VCR. Isn't it great?'' I took note of the new VCR and wondered if the purchase coincided with the robbery. ''When we get enough money saved, he's taking me to a clinic in Mexico, where they're going to help me so that I can think better.''

As motives went, Brad's didn't seem to be an evil one. Nevertheless, I couldn't quite reconcile this picture of compassionate artist and loving brother with someone who could drive down an old friend in the street and leave him to die.

I was about to finagle a tour of the apartment when a loud horn called from the lot outside. I peered out the window and saw Gary and Charli gazing up at me. Closer to the building, Brad Paladin was locking his Pinto. Apparently, he'd gotten off work early.

''I'll see you around,'' I told Brad's sister, as I hastened for the door.

''Thank you,'' she said nicely. ''Do you want a tip?''

I barely heard her. I pounded down the stairs and gained the first floor just as Brad began walking up the sidewalk. Buzzing around the stairwell, I trotted to the back of the building. I burst out the back door.

Gary and Charli were waiting in the Le Baron at the curb. Without speaking, I leapt into the car. Gary slammed down the accelerator. We barreled out of the lot.

"Seat belt," he said, as I fought the centrifugal force slamming me into the seat.

I was already working it. Expecting a harangue, I was delighted when Gary offered me a huge grin and said, "Find out what you needed? Did I do all right?"

"You did great, honey," I answered, reaching for his cheek. He tilted his head and planted a kiss in the palm of my hand, never decelerating. For all the world, I felt like Bonnie to Gary's Clyde.

I took my hat off and let my hair ripple in the breeze. Adrenaline still coursed through my system. Close calls are so exhilarating. I figured that I now had a motive for Brad to rob, steal, and possibly murder. Responsibility for his sister could not have been easy.

As Gary swung the car into the driveway of my house, I tipped my head back, looked at the limitless sky, and yelled, "Where are they?"

"Where are what?" Gary said, laughing, leaning against his car door.

"The fourth-edition Fuzzy Wuzzies. If we can find the fourth edition, we find our murderer." Brad could have them in the apartment. Dick Chase could have them. Persons unknown could have them. Perhaps Gladys Zimmerman had gotten hold of them and she only pretended to partner with me to throw me off guard.

Gary reached across the seats and fingered a tendril of my hair. "Whom do you think might have them?" he asked, as though he were genuinely trying to help.

I ran down the list, which included Mary, Victor, or Lizzie, who might have discovered the valuable property and made use of that knowledge. I also told him what I considered to be the most likely scenario.

"How are you going to find out who it is?" Gary asked, his tone not quite so jovial.

"I have a plan," I announced.

"A plan."

"Yes. A foolproof plan. By this time Sunday, we'll know who has the Fuzzies, who killed Gene, and why." I grinned.

He didn't answer me, and he didn't look happy at all.

Chapter Fifteen

For the next few days, I was a very busy woman. Sue had a few papers for me to sign in regards to the house. I tied up some details about my next sale. And, for good measure, I began composing my reply to the Melody Joy gallery. Primarily, I strove to prepare for a gathering that I was hosting. A ''suspect soirée,'' so to speak. Everyone who was anyone would be there. And by the time we cut the cake, I'd have my killer in cuffs.

The cuffs part would be tricky. Since I'm not a police officer, the final details of my crime fighting require a bit of professional backup. No way would Cole be coerced into such risky business. Fortunately, I knew someone who could be . . . with the right incentive.

*   *   *

"Bogert," Phil said, as she dipped her roller into a pan of powder-blue paint. The rental house smelled of ammonia and lemon and cigarette memories. "What makes you think that I want any part of another of your harebrained schemes?" She neglected to roll off enough of the excess paint, and the stuff lightly splattered her face when she tried to apply it to the ceiling.

"Because," I replied happily, walking around the small living room checking out the rest of her rental, "we have so much history together. We're going to be neighbors." I saved the best for last. "And if this works, we'll solve another one of Cole's cases. Don't you think it's our duty to keep his 'mega mucho macho mini'?"

She turned away, but not before I detected her smile. If Phil was anything, it was competitive, and T. J. Cole was her first real competition for the position of finest of Landview's finest.

"Conditions," Phil said, placing the roller in the pan and walking to the four-paned window that faced my back deck.

"Yeeess?" I didn't like the sound of this.

"No wacky parties with your weird friends."

"No wacky parties with my weird friends . . . too often," I deadpanned.

Before she could ask—and I felt pretty sure that her pride wouldn't allow her to—I offered. "I could babysit Dot sometimes when you are working."

"I wouldn't trust you with my pet hamster, let alone my daughter," Phil sniped. Nevertheless, I perceived a quiver of relief in her tight shoulders. Things couldn't be easy for her with Tommy apparently out of the picture for good.

"Only in emergencies, of course," I hastened to add.

"Emergencies..." she mused. "Okay, Bogert. You've got yourself a deal."

I sighed. "The usual terms?"

She grinned. "Yep. If it works out, I get the glory. If it doesn't, you get the blame."

We shook hands on it.

Back at home, I made a few phone calls. I needed room reservations (a suite at the Chicago Hilton), a certain businessman for my leading man, and Gladys Zimmerman to be my date for the "event."

Messenger-delivered notes went to Mary Waite and Brad Paladin.

Of course, Dad and Jewel wanted in on the finale. I decided to let Jewel cater the affair and allow Dad to help her deliver the hors d'oeuvres. That left Gary.

"I'm not sure that I like you doing this," he said, after seeing a movie together Friday night. We were parked in my driveway and I was nestled within the crook of his arm. "Why don't you leave it to the police?"

Irritation ruined the moment. Intellectually, I understood that his question was born out of concern, yet I'd spent too much time believing that he had controlled and manipulated me in our former relationship to let go of that suspicion entirely now.

"At least, can't you wait until I get back from Indianapolis?'' Gary had an important sales convention over the weekend.

''Nope,'' I said, deciding to ignore my rush of indignation. ''Go sell some computers. When you get back, we'll celebrate the conclusion of the Fuzzy Wuzzy case. I'll . . .''

His hands gripped the steering wheel and he gazed at nothing straight ahead. ''Be careful, Kathryn Bogert,'' he said solemnly.

''I will.''

''I'm not done with you yet.''

''I'm glad.''

He took me in his arms and kissed me. Any doubts I had fled on a rush of delight. Oh, how I'd missed this.

What to wear? What to wear? Saturday evening I studied my wardrobe with Charli at my feet. I'd already chosen a thick black leather collar with silver studs for his duds. The spikes made him look really tough. *Oh, what the heck?* ''We might as well be a pair, eh, buddy?''

It didn't take me long to finish dressing. By the time my date arrived, I'd donned black leather pants, a Harley T-shirt, a black leather jacket, and a black cap in place. I checked my reflection in the mirror and saw someone who'd look right at home on the back of Cole's motorcycle. Biker chick and her dog. Cool.

Gladys Zimmerman took one look at me and nearly exploded. ''What kind of a getup is that? You screw

this up, and missy, you're going to be popping whee-
lies ten feet under!''

''Don't worry about it,'' I told her. I pulled my
jacket to the side and offered a quick glimpse of a
shoulder holster and a really authentic-looking trick
gun I'd picked up at the Pawlicki sale. She didn't have
to know it was fake. ''One way or the other, we get
the money.''

She looked at me with grudging admiration and
walked ahead to her car. By the time we were on our
way, I was praying that we'd miss the rush hour and
that all the other players would, too. Jewel and Dad
had left hours ago. Timing was critical.

''So how did you happen to stumble onto this
buyer?'' Gladys asked. She drove like her Plymouth
was a tank crossing de Gaulle's France: determinedly,
mullingly, obtusely.

''When I located the Fuzzies,'' I replied, patting the
sealed carton next to me, ''the pawn shop had already
been contacted by some of their regular customers
about an out-of-towner looking to make a buy. I was
lucky that I'd gotten there first.''

''I don't know why you won't show them to me,''
she said, surly, disembarking the Dan Ryan for North
Lake Shore Drive.

''I told you. I packaged them tightly for security.
Trust me. They're the real thing. And you're going to
get your share real soon.''

Charli poked me in the shoulder with his snout. I
couldn't tell if it was a gesture of criticism or praise.

* * *

The Chicago Hilton, on Michigan Avenue, remains one of the truly beautiful hotels in Chicago. With its jazz bars, upscale shops, and Grand Ballroom, it caters to the select consumer. I'd decided that it would be perfect for tonight's activities. The concierge looked askance at Charli and me and Gladys, who had worn her Wards polyester, but she gave us the room number that we requested.

"This guy is expecting us?" Gladys asked. She seemed a bit uncomfortable in the elevator, as though she might be a tad claustrophobic.

"It's all set," I said slyly, balancing the box on my hip. "We'll be in and out in no time."

A knock on the door of Room 4003 brought an answering summons. "Come in," a man said courteously. I struggled to keep my cool as Dick Chase led us across a spacious room to where Hugh Rogers lounged on a plush sofa. A tumbler of something amber rested in his hand. The appetizers Jewel had prepared lay sumptuously across the coffee table in front of him, lending an air of elegance to the occasion. Hugh gave no indication that he recognized me. I followed his lead.

Gladys gazed about the room, obviously ill at ease. She straightened her skirt, cleared her throat, and said, "So you're interested in buying."

Dick's eyes gleamed with something I didn't like.

"I might be." Hugh could play poker. His steady gaze never left her face. He took a sharp swallow of his drink.

"Well," Gladys said, "if you're not, there are others who are."

"Let's see the merchandise," Hugh said, leaning forward and placing his tumbler on the table beside a platter of stuffed Portabellas. Dick had taken up residence over by a faux-marble fireplace. His casual stance was at odds with his attentiveness.

Before either of us could reply, another knock sounded at the door. Dick went over to answer it. I was not surprised to see Mary Waite. After all, I had invited her with an anonymous note telling her that if she wanted to know what had happened to Gene that she should come to the Hilton at precisely 7:45—no cops. Apparently, she'd chosen to bring Victor. Excellent. He looked around the room disdainfully and held her elbow possessively.

"You," Mary cried when she saw me. "What are you doing here?"

Mary was no dummy. She studied everyone for a moment before continuing. "I demand an explanation. I will not be toyed with."

Hugh looked prepared to ask Dick to throw the intruders out. Before he could do so, Lizzie popped up behind her mother. "Don't act so innocent, Mother. I knew if I followed you long enough, you'd do something stupid. These are your fellow conspirators, aren't they?"

She swept a disgusted look over my leather. "Well," she cried, "I'm not leaving until I know how Father died."

Gladys darted glances at Mary, me, the box, Hugh. I could see her thinking hard and coming up confused.

Before anyone could say anything further, I pulled my "gun."

"Never mind, Lizzie." Gladys gasped. Mary's eyes narrowed. Victor looked ready to spit nails. Hugh and Dick registered controlled alarm. I gestured with the gun. "All of you. Away from the door. Now. Keep your hands up in the air."

"Bogert, what are you doing?" Gladys cried. "What . . ."

Dick made as if to ignore me. Charli growled, deep and menacingly. Dick complied with my request. The dog sort of herded this unlikely group into a bunch by the huge glass window overlooking the street. I made my way to a lamp by the sofa and turned it down to a faint glow. "Quiet," I ordered everyone as I backtracked to the door. "Don't move. Be quiet and you won't get hurt."

A soft knock sounded from the other side of the door. I didn't take my gun off the group, instead gesturing with my free hand for them to maintain silence.

Another knock.

I could feel my heart pounding in my chest. Perspiration threatened to make me my grip on the gun. Where was Phil?

The room hummed with tension. I knew I couldn't hold this group at bay for long. Suddenly, the sound of a lock being tampered with pierced the silence.

Out of the corner of my eye, I watched the door swing open. The exaggerated silhouette of a man appeared framed by the corridor's light. Charli padded silently across the room. I reached for the lamp and turned up its power. A blare of white light momentarily blinded Brad Paladin. Not so me. I saw the glint of his revolver with chilling clarity. The guy had a lot of guns.

He recovered instantly and brought his weapon down to face mine.

"Good of you to come," I said, imitating a calm that I did not feel.

His squirrel eyes darted around the room, taking in everything and obviously understanding nothing—except that he'd stepped into a trap.

"Drop the gun," he told me. His hand quit shaking. He focused completely on me now, as though he'd decided to deal with the others later.

"No," I replied.

"Are you nuts?" Gladys cried. "Drop the gun."

"I don't think so." I held my ground. "Brad. I know that you hijacked the fourth edition and killed Gene. I don't care about the old guy, but I want those toys. Now."

"Doublecrosser," Gladys muttered at me.

"Gene?" Mary Waite said in a voice that sounded so pained it was as though someone had knifed her. I sensed Lizzie move closer to her mother and slip her arm around the woman.

"I'm prepared to pay good money for those Fuzzies," Hugh said nonchalantly. "A good deal more than any of these others."

"I don't know what you're talking about," Brad said, his left eye squinting slightly.

"I think you do," I said. I walked to a spot beside the bedroom door where I could pivot and cover both Brad and the others. "You intercepted the Fuzzies at the loading docks of the Lucky Dish Factory."

"The Lucky Dish?" Hugh roared and turned to his son-in-law.

"She's lying, Hugh. I don't have any idea what this is about."

"You asked Gene to hide them for you," I went on, struggling to maintain control of the situation. "And then, when you were ready to sell, you arranged to meet him. He gave you the goods, but that wasn't enough. You didn't want to split the money. You ran him over and left him for dead."

"No," Brad said, his hand shaking once again. His gaze darted from me to Chase to the Waites. "That's not how it went down."

"It didn't?" I said snidely. "And I suppose you didn't rob that White Hen and stow the weapon in Gene's basement. I suppose that you didn't burn down the house, hoping to destroy all evidence of just how often you had abused the trust Gene had in you . . . right up until the very end."

Dick Chase somehow harnessed some of the leadership ability that must have gotten him elected president of the park district. "Give me the gun, Ms. Bogert," he said seductively, stepping closer. "I'll see that he doesn't get away."

Panic contorted Brad's face. He nearly dropped his

weapon. Collecting himself, he targeted Chase and said, ''Stop, right there. Don't come any closer.''

''That's not how it happened,'' Brad began, talking as if to all of us.

''Shut up,'' Dick cried. Another step.

''No.'' Brad swiped at some perspiration dripping down his cheek. ''I did steal the Fuzzies. A box fell open at the docks. I knew that they were worth something, so I brought them to Gene. I would have shared any profit with him.''

Dick Chase dove across the room, barreling into Brad's legs. The other man's gun went off. The shot went wild, striking a vase on the mantle.

Three things happened at once.

''Charli,'' I cried. The dog, who had been growling in the back of his throat, burst forward. Snapping his mouth over Brad's gun arm, his teeth pressed into the flesh. Phil burst out of the bedroom, service revolver braced in ready position. Cole kicked open the door from the hall.

''Police!'' the two detectives cried simultaneously. ''Drop your weapon!''

Brad's gun fell to the floor. Chase pulled his arm back as though to deliver a knockout punch. Not a chance. Hugh strode across the room and grabbed his son-in-law by the wrist. Yanking hard, he hauled Chase to his feet. ''I didn't want to believe it. First, that you would steal that collection out from under me and second, that you could have had anything to do with that man's death.''

''You were in on this?'' Dick Chase raged. His face

was florid with anger. I wasn't sure for a moment if he would ignore the weapons directed at him and assault Hugh.

"Charli." I called the dog over and harnessed my "gun." "Good boy. Good job, Charli." I stopped next to him and stroked his fur around that spiked collar.

"It's true," Brad said, "that I asked Gene to meet me. But I didn't run him over. I wasn't even supposed to be there. Chase said that he'd forget about my taking his stuff if I just made arrangements for him to get the merchandise back. I didn't trust him. I went to the pick-up anyway."

Dick Chase stiffened. His eyes widened and then sort of glazed over.

"I saw it." Brad pointed and sniffled. "I saw everything. Gene stepped into the street and Chase ran him over. He drove right over him and never came back."

"You're wrong," Chase muttered. "Waite dropped something. It rolled into the street. Waite went after it. It was too late for me to stop. It was an accident, I tell you. It was an accident."

For a moment, no one said anything. The room was so thick with emotion that I felt nearly smothered by it. Mary's grief. Brad's desperation. Hugh's outrage. Lizzie's shock.

"Just happen to be in the neighborhood, Cole?" Phil asked handcuffing Brad.

"Mary Waite called me despite the warning in her note. What's your excuse?" Cole replied, as he did the same to Dick Chase.

"Just a favor for a friend," Phil said. I swear she winked at me.

Gladys had plunked herself down on the sofa and was helping herself to a hearty glass of booze. Victor attempted to lead Mary to the security of a chair. Lizzie nearly slapped his hands and instead escorted her mother herself. "Do you need some water, Mother?" Lizzie asked with apparent sincerity.

Mary struggled for control and nodded finally. She grasped her daughter's hand. They both seemed to just hold on.

Victor sat next to Gladys and sullenly began eating some petits fours and the arrest continued without any further help from me.

"Thank you, Hugh," I told the Texan. I'd suspected his son's guilt and had hoped that I was wrong. "I'm sorry about Dick."

"I'm sorry, too. But I thank you, young lady. It's about time that I took little Becky and gave her a little discipline and a lot of love."

Thinking about his granddaughter, I couldn't agree more.

"Do you think it really was an accident?" A familiar voice brought my head upright with a snap. Dad stood in the doorway with Jewel.

"What close up are you two doing here?" I cried.

Jewel looked a bit shamefaced. "Well, now, as long as we were here, we sort of booked a room for the night."

"And hung around to make sure that my girl didn't

bite off more than she could chew,'' Dad added, shaking his finger at me.

They looked so sweet together. I couldn't help hoping that with my imminent move and Jewel finishing her teaching stint that Dad would finally get around to proposing. Everything would be perfect then.

A clawlike hand grasped my arm. I gazed down into the somewhat sloppy face of Gladys Zimmerman. She belched. ''I knew you'd noodle things out. That's why I hung that disgusting Fuzzy from your porch and 'partnered' with you. Nobody was going to bump off Gene and get off scot-free. Good work, Bogert.'' She slapped me hard across the back. I nearly bit my tongue off.

As Gladys wove her way back to the bracing support of another drink, Jewel asked me, ''Do you think it really was an accident? Do you think that Dick Chase didn't run over Gene on purpose?''

''That'll be for the courts to decide, Jewel,'' Dad replied sagely. ''Hey, where's Charli? I think his outfit would look great for December's pin-up. A motorcycle Christmas.''

Jewel laughed and pointed to the coffee table repast. ''I wish Gary were here to capture that image.''

Charli looked up, his jowls dripping caviar. She was right. It would make a cute photo, and I confess, I rather wished Gary were here myself.

''No sense in letting all this food go to waste,'' Dad said, moving to join the dog. They were used to dining together.

I shook my head. We were quite a collection, those of us left in the room. Not so rare, perhaps, as the infamous fourth edition, but definitely worth keeping an eye on. For certainly love, loyalty, and family could only appreciate in value.